The Missing Millionaire

ALSO BY ROGER SILVERWOOD

The
MISSING
MILLIONAIRE

ROGER SILVERWOOD

JOFFE BOOKS

Revised edition 2025
Joffe Books, London
www.joffebooks.com

First published as *The Man Who Couldn't Lose*
in Great Britain in 2007

This paperback edition was first published
in Great Britain in 2025

Cover art by Nick Castle

ISBN: 978-1-80573-186-3

ONE

Bromersley, South Yorkshire, UK
18 October 1970, 23.15 hours

The young couple were in the dark, sheltered archway of the Theatre Royal on Bradford Street, leaning against the closed emergency-exit door. The second house had long since finished. The theatre had emptied. The lights were out. The street was deserted.

His arms were round her, and he pressed his hard body against her and gave her a long, tender kiss. When their lips parted, she sighed, and ran a hand through his hair. He was a big, strong, athletic young man with a distinctive lined face.

'Joshua,' she whispered breathily.

Through the darkness he could just see the whites of her big eyes. He sighed, smiled, pulled her back to him and nuzzled into her hair while his fingers eagerly explored her vertebrae; at the same time, she rubbed her hands up and down his arms and shoulders. The only sound to be heard was the heavy breathing and pounding of their hearts. Their loving thoughts were turning to ecstatic dreams as they floated gently in each other's arms.

Suddenly, there was the loud bang of a door being shut, close by, followed by a rattle of keys, then the sound of heavy shoes on stone steps.

They came back abruptly to earth. They froze in the dark shadow of the doorway, hoping not to be discovered.

Someone had come out of the front door of the theatre and was standing on the pavement.

They turned and edged forward. They could just see his outline in the moonlight. He was a portly man in a long coat. At the same moment, a car raced up seemingly from nowhere and stopped at the door with a squeal of brakes. The driver got out, leaving the engine running, and came round to the theatre door. The headlights showed him to be a slim man in a light-coloured raincoat.

The young couple, only twelve feet away from the car, held on to each other motionless, yet listening, wishing the two men would go away and leave them undisturbed.

'You are late,' the hard voice of the younger man began quietly.

'Got held up.'

'Got the money?'

'Got the stuff?'

'Yes.'

'Where is it?'

'In the boot.'

'Show me.'

There were footsteps to the back of the car. There was a click of a catch as the boot lid was raised.

'Where?'

There was no reply.

Suddenly, there was a gasp and the older man said, 'What's that? No!' he said urgently. There was fear in his voice.

The younger man's voice hardened.

'Drop the money in the back and step away from the car.'

'No.'

'Do as I tell you.'

'If you pull that trigger, you'll waken half the town. The cops'll be here in no time.'

'I mean it. Do as I say.'

'You wouldn't dare.'

'Put that down! Stand back!'

'No.'

'Drop it or I shoot.'

Then there was the clatter of metal hitting metal, the whooshing of a .202 leaving the barrel of a Walther PPX fitted with a silencer, the rattle of an iron bar clattering on the road, followed by the sound of two men slumping to the ground.

The young couple in the shadows of the doorway stood motionless, their lungs tight with air.

The only sound to be heard was the ticking of the car engine.

The young man disentangled himself from the girl and peered round the corner of the doorway.

'What's happened?' she whispered.

'Stay there, Myra.'

Joshua looked down at the two men. One lay on top of the other. They were motionless. An iron bar lay on the road, reflecting the light.

He licked his lips. Then stepped gingerly out from the safe cover of the doorway onto the pavement. He looked up and then down the short street. All was quiet. The noise of the pistol shot didn't seem to have disturbed anybody. He leaned over the two men and rubbed his chin. He touched the neck of the younger man, searching for a pulse. His fingers felt hot and sticky. He was touching blood. It was oozing out of the man's head and running down his neck. Joshua gasped. He unrolled the man's fingers from round the Walther PPX and shoved it into his pocket. He picked up a brown paper parcel from the road and threw it in the car boot. Then he went deftly through his pockets and found a wallet. He pushed the younger man off the top of the other man with his foot and then swiftly crouched down and lifted his wallet from his inside pocket.

He saw Myra's feet. She was standing next to him, hands in her pockets.

'Are they dead, Joshua?' she said.

He looked up at her.

'Yes,' he said quickly.

'Oh,' she gasped. 'Are you sure?'

'Get in the car.'

'Where's the nearest phone?'

'Get in the car,' he snapped. 'Hurry up.'

'What you going to do? Aren't you going to phone the police?'

'*Get in the car!*' he bawled.

They heard the clatter of footsteps running in the distance.

His pulse raced.

Myra hesitated.

'What you doing?' she said, her eyes flashing.

Joshua opened the car door.

'This is our chance!' he yelled.

He pushed her into the car.

The running footsteps were louder.

4

Joshua dashed round the rear of the car, skirting the two bodies and accidentally kicking the iron bar as he scrambled to the driver's door.

Lights inside the foyer of the theatre burst into life. The silhouette of a man's head and shoulders was framed in the glass door.

Joshua saw him and it made him catch his breath. His heart pounded.

He slammed the car door shut; his hands were shaking.

'There's somebody coming,' Myra squealed.

He fumbled in the dark to find the clutch, the gear stick and then the handbrake; the big car jerked with a loud squeal of rubber away from the kerb into the night.

* * *

Sebastopol Terrace, Bromersley, South Yorkshire, UK
19 March 2007, 13.15 hours

Joshua Gumme, sitting in the back of the Bentley, pressed a button on the armrest and lowered the internal privacy window behind the driver.

'Stop here. Number thirteen. This is the one, Horace,' he growled.

'Yes, Mr Gumme.'

'Hurry up and get my chair out.'

'Yes, Mr Gumme.'

Horace 'Harelip' Makepiece pulled on the handbrake of the Bentley outside the little terraced house and switched off the ignition. He dashed out of the driver's seat, slammed the door, rushed to the rear of the limo, opened the tailgate and lifted out a wheelchair. He bounced the wheels on the pavement, pressed down the seat to open it and make it rigid and then manoeuvred it up to the nearside rear door of the car.

Joshua Gumme, immaculately dressed in a plain clerical grey three-piece suit, white shirt, dark tie and black Homburg, smart as paint but forty years out of date, swung his large frame out of the car on to the wheelchair and immediately rolled the wheels impatiently towards the door of the little house.

Makepiece closed the boot and the car door and dashed across the pavement to grab hold of the wheelchair handles.

They were soon at the house door. They didn't have to knock. It was swiftly opened by a slim young woman in a shapeless dress, sloppy sandals and with mousey-coloured hair, a clump of it flopping across one cheek. She was wearing a delicately carved necklace comprising twenty or more small heart-shaped garnets, each in a delicate old gold setting and connected by pretty leaf motif chain links. Her face was red and sweaty; her eyes were tired. The chatter of children and occasionally playful screaming could be heard from the kitchen behind her.

'Yes?' she said commandingly, looking down at Gumme in the chair then glancing at Makepiece standing behind. 'You're back again. What you want? My husband's out, looking for work. And if you're wanting money, we haven't got any.'

Gumme's lips tightened. He cleared his throat.

'Young lady,' he began sternly.

She put her hands on her hips and said, 'We're never going to be able to pay you anymore, Mr Gumme.'

'Mrs Tasker,' he said icily. His eyes suddenly alighted on the garnet and gold necklace twinkling slightly on her white chest. His eyes narrowed as he looked at it but he said nothing. He looked quickly up into her face.

'Yes. I'm Mrs Tasker,' she said proudly. 'And I've got two children to show for it. And my husband can't possibly pay you.'

'Yes, well,' he replied, rubbing his chin. 'We'll see about that. I'll come back when your husband's in,' he said curtly.

'He's out looking for work,' she said, running the tip of her tongue lightly across her lips.

He looked back at Makepiece and waggled a finger.

'Give her a card,' he snapped.

Makepiece whisked out his wallet, found a business card and passed it over to Mrs Tasker.

She wrinkled her nose as she took it.

'Tell him to phone me at that number, tonight, Muriel,' Gumme said, staring hard into her face. 'Tonight!' he repeated loudly. Then he whisked the wheelchair through 180 degrees, dragging Makepiece round with him, and pushed the wheels vigorously towards the car.

Muriel Tasker shivered and felt her pulse quicken. She went back inside the house, closed the door and leaned back against it, breathing unevenly with a hand on her chest.

* * *

Doncaster Rail Station
South Yorkshire, UK
20 March 2007, 08.40 hours

The voice on the tannoy bawled out, '*The train arriving on Platform One is the 6.05 from King's Cross.*'

A few people were waiting on the platform to greet it. Among them was a big man who was leaning against a pillar in front of the waiting room reading the *Sporting Life*. As the train rolled in, he stuffed the newspaper into his jacket pocket and stepped forward.

Carriage after carriage rolled past with passengers gathering at the doors.

The train squealed to a halt.

At one door, a severe-looking man in large black hat, clerical collar and black suit, carrying a large black case, an umbrella and a black book inscribed in gold leaf with the words 'Holy Bible', descended the steps.

The big man saw him and rushed forward. He looked round to see who was near and then, in a loud voice, said, 'Are you Father Ignatius of the Little Brothers Of The Poor?'

The man in the black suit and the clerical collar smiled graciously down at him and said, 'Indeed I am, my son.'

The man nodded and returned the smile. He didn't know why. He didn't feel like smiling.

Out of the corner of his mouth, the man in black said, 'Why don't you offer to take my suitcase, you great lump-head?'

The big man's eyes froze momentarily. He knew not to mess with the man in the black hat.

'Oh. Can I take your case, good Father?' he stammered loudly.

'Very well, my dear friend,' the man replied with a show of teeth and a flourish of the hand. 'I am sure that your kindness to a humble cleric will be rewarded in heaven.'

'Oh?' He blinked and bowed. 'Yes, sir. Thank you. This way, Father.'

The big man bustled along the underpass with the case, and up the steps through the ticket barrier to a car waiting outside, while the man in black strode slowly and deliberately behind him in his own time, gripping the Bible in one hand and using the umbrella as a walking stick. The big man unlocked the car, put the case in the car boot, then opened the front nearside door for the man and waited by it. The man in black ignored the open door and instead opened the offside rear door. He wedged the umbrella between the seats, climbed into the car and, nursing the Bible on his lap, reached out and closed the door. The big man, seeing what had happened, closed the door, ran round the car and got in the driver's seat.

Once they were on their way, the man in black said, 'Now remember, you always call me Father Ignatius. OK?'

'Whatever you say, boss,' he said, without thinking.

The eyes of the man in black glowed like hot cinders. His fists tightened. 'I said you call me Father Ignatius, you bloody idiot!' he hissed like a snake about to bite.

When the driver realized what he'd said, his blood turned to ice. He licked his lips and gripped the steering wheel more tightly.

'Sorry, sir. Father Ignatius, I mean.'

The man in black sighed heavily.

They travelled the ten miles to Bromersley in silence. It was only when the driver stopped outside the front door of the Feathers Hotel that the man in the cleric's clothes said, 'Now listen, son. And listen good. You know nothing about me. If you are asked by the police, or anybody else, all you know about me is that my name is Father Ignatius and that I come from Ireland. That's all you need to know. If I find you've been shooting your mouth off, I shall come looking for you. Understand?'

The man's blood ran cold. He sat in the driver's seat as still as a corpse and wished he was anywhere but there.

'Yes. Sure. Father Ignatius.'

'Right. And don't phone me. *Never* phone me. If I need *you*, I'll contact you. Right?'

'Right. Yes. Sure, Father Ignatius.'

He slammed the car door and shot into The Feathers.

The driver watched him swish through the revolving doors. He sighed, grabbed himself a can of Grolsch from under the dash, tore off the ring pull, slung it through the window, took a big swig from the can and then hopped out the car to open the boot as the hotel porter appeared.

There was a card on the lift doors that read, 'Out Of Order', but old Walter, the hotel porter, wasted no time and bustled up the stairs with the suitcase to room 102, closely followed by the man in black.

The old man led him into the room, put his luggage on the case stand and said, 'Dinner is served from six until eight-thirty, and room service is all day until ten o'clock. Will there be anything else, sir?'

'No, thank you, my son,' he replied with a flash of teeth. Then he opened the cover of the Bible and took out a small card about two inches by four inches. It had a beautifully printed colour picture of an angel on one side and the words 'May the good Lord preserve you and keep you' on the other.

'There you are,' he said, handing it to the old man.

Walter gawped at him and took the card. He stared at it.

'Never neglect to say your prayers each night, my son, and you are certain to go to heaven and enjoy the fruits of paradise.'

Walter had never met a character like this before. Unusually, he was lost for words.

'Yes, sir. I will, sir. Thank you, sir.'

He handed him the room key and went out.

As soon as the door was closed, the man rushed over to it, inserted the key and locked it. He then dashed across to the window, peered out of it then ran to the bathroom, checked that it was empty, and tried the window but it wouldn't budge. Came back into the bedroom, looked in the wardrobe and then under the bed.

Then he sat on the edge of the bed and sighed.

After a moment, he threw down the Bible, dragged his hat and wig off, scratched his bald head vigorously for thirty seconds, and unfastened his collar and let it hang loose.

Then he reached out for the Bible. He opened it, took out the Smith and Wesson .38 from the cut-out cavity and pushed it under the pillow.

* * *

Bromersley, South Yorkshire, UK
20 March 2007, 22.50 hours

Peace and quiet descended on Edmondson's Avenue, a quiet street of semi-detached houses on the new council estate on the Barnsley side of Bromersley. The landlord of The Fat Duck on the corner had long since called 'Time, gentlemen, please', Fletcher's fish and chip shop had sold out and emptied the deep fat fryer, and Mr Patel at the off licence had sold the last six-pack of Carling for the night and cashed up. Most residents had switched off their televisions. Dogs had been let in and cats put out. Doors had been locked and barred and lights extinguished. In fact, it was as quiet as death and as black as a joiner's thumbnail.

A man in a dark raincoat made his way swiftly and noiselessly along the street to the red post-box, outside number twenty-six. There was a small light from the hallway showing through the front-room window. He opened the paling gate and made his way down the concrete path round the side of the house to the back, tapped three times lightly on the door, waited a second then tapped three times more. The light in the house went out and the door opened. The man slipped inside and quickly closed and locked the door behind him. Then the light went on to reveal a big woman standing behind him. She had one hand on the light switch and the other holding a glass, half filled with a clear liquid.

On the kitchen table was a bottle of Polish vodka, a glass and a bowl of ice cubes.

The man turned round from locking the door, his eyes flitted round the little room blinking in the bright light.

He noticed the window.

'Draw the curtains, Gloria, for God's sake.'

She pursed her lips.

'There's nobody around at this time,' she said, looking closely at him with a sour face.

'There might be, you never know.'

He pulled a small parcel out of his raincoat pocket and put it on the table.

'Your mother in bed?'

'Yes.'

'Is she all right?'

'I s'pose,' she sniffed. 'She's tired. Thank God. Been out all day gallivanting . . . on a church trip.' She picked up a giant teddy bear by its ear off a chair. 'Came back with this. Won it in a raffle,' she said sourly.

He glanced at it and wrinkled his nose.

'Are you sure she doesn't know what's going on?'

She smiled wryly and plonked the teddy bear back on the chair.

'All she's interested in is her bowels and the church.'

She shrugged, put her glass down, crossed over to the sink and pulled the plastic curtain across to cut out the night sky.

He sat down and began dropping ice cubes in the glass. Then he unscrewed the cap on the vodka bottle and began to pour.

He looked up at her, screwed up his eyes and took a sip from the glass.

Gloria went to a cutlery drawer and took out a thick wodge of bank notes, tidily sorted and held together by an elastic band. She tossed it in front of him.

'Four thousand pounds,' she said with a sniff, a toss of the head and a smirk.

The man smiled, picked it up, shook it at her and smiled again.

She folded her arms and smiled back.

'Four thousand,' he said, throwing it down on the table. 'One day's work.'

He shook his head in incredulity and took a celebratory swig.

She sat at the table opposite him. She emptied her glass and began to refill it with ice from the bowl.

'Any trouble?'

She shook her head.

'Like candy off a baby.'

He looked down at the money. He licked his bottom lip. He rubbed his chin. Then his face changed from delight to concern.

Gloria noticed.

'What's the matter?'

'We'll have to cut back, Gloria,' he said, shaking his head and rubbing his chin. 'It's too much. You'll be creating too much traffic. They'll notice . . . or someone will squeal. And you'll be raided.'

'That's up to you,' she said. 'I'd sooner go on. Can't go on for ever. You never know when it'll all end. But I'll tell you this,' she said, pointing a mean finger at his eyes. 'I'm not going into Holloway for you or anybody else. I couldn't stand it at my age, and it would kill my mother.'

He nodded. He understood her concern. He had worries of his own. He ran his hand through his hair.

'Look, I've told you. If you get a phone call, take all the stuff, every last twist of it, and all the money . . . don't keep *any* back. If you've hidden any they'll find it, and you'd have to account for it, and remember, you're supposed to be a hard-up widow woman struggling to keep your mother on a pension. It'll not do if they find you with a crafty thousand quid stuffed up your knicker leg. They'll search *you* as well, you know.'

She glared at him. Her lips tightened across her teeth. She put her hands on her hips.

'Let any man come near to search me,' she said menacingly, 'and he'll never do it again.'

'That's what we've got big, fat policewomen for.'

'Hmm,' she said, pulling a sour face.

'Put it in that self-seal bag in the drawer. And do as I've told you.'

'I know. I know.'

'Believe me, if that or the money is on the premises or even buried in the garden, they'd find it.'

They both drank in silence for a few moments, looking down at the white tablecloth for no good reason.

She noticed the parcel again and nodded towards it.

'How much have you brought?'

'Should make eight thousand,' he said and pulled the parcel across in front of her.

She sniffed.

'Two days' worth.'

She wrinkled her nose.

'Then we'll take a break,' he said.

She pulled a face then shook her head. 'The punters'll still keep coming.'

'Tell them you can't get the stuff. It'll make them keener. You can open up again in a week or so.'

'They'll go somewhere else.'

'They'll be back,' he shouted confidently and lifted the glass.

'Shhh!' Gloria hissed. 'You'll waken my mother.'

TWO

The Police Station, Bromersley, South Yorkshire
21 March 2007, 10.00 hours

The sun was shining, the sky was cloudless, the birds were singing, the villains were counting money, their wives were at the beauty shop getting new fingernails, their offspring were getting legless while being tattooed, their Rottweilers were barking in their gardens and Detective Inspector Angel was in his office, humming, 'Oh what a beautiful morning . . . Oh what a beautiful day . . . I've got that wonderful feeling . . . Everything's going my way.'

He was packing a cardboard box that had the word Weetabix printed on each side of it, with the statements, tape transcriptions, exhibits, forensic report and photographs connected with the murders of two showgirls, Fiona Frinton and Imelda Wilde. It had been a most difficult case that he had eventually solved; the murderer had been arrested and was safely on remand awaiting trial. In the box was the entire case for the prosecution, for delivery next door to Oliver

Twelvetrees, leading barrister at the CPS. Angel had taped up the box lid and was pressing down the gummed addressed label on the top when the telephone rang.

He frowned, looked thoughtfully at the machine then leaned over and picked it up.

'Angel,' he said brightly.

It was the civilian woman telephone receptionist.

'There's a Mrs Buller-Price, I think her name is, on the line asking for you, Inspector,' she said tentatively. 'She sounds a bit . . . distressed. Will you speak to her?'

'Of course. Of course,' he said promptly. He never refused to speak to anyone who called asking for him by name. He always said that they might want to pass on information that might help solve a crime. In this instance, it was Mrs Buller-Price, an old friend of Angel's. She was a dear, kind widow who kept a small farm at Tunistone, on the Pennines six miles out of Bromersley. He had known her for years. In all circumstances, he would never have declined to speak to her.

'I'm putting her through.'

'Ah. Is that dear Inspector Angel?' Mrs Buller-Price said. She always spoke in a most genteel voice. This morning she seemed particularly agitated.

'Indeed it is,' he said reassuringly. 'Good morning to you, Mrs Buller-Price.'

'Oh dear. Oh dear,' she said quickly.

Angel realized that something was wrong.

'Now whatever is the matter?'

'Oh dear, dear Inspector. I am sorry to bother you, but I have been burgled.'

'Burgled?' he said angrily.

'Yes. Someone has been in the house and taken my teapot money, two hundred pounds, my silver photograph frames, the pearls my husband bought me, my emerald ring and ear-rings . . . and . . . I don't know what else.'

'Oh dear, I am sorry. When was this?'

'Must have been yesterday. I was out yesterday afternoon, you see. Got back about eight last evening, and I didn't notice. This morning, the pantry door was rattling. I went in to investigate. I thought it was unusually cool and draughty in there. It was then that I saw the window had been smashed. Then I looked around and realized that I had been burgled.'

'Well, don't touch anything. I'll send—'

'Oh, Inspector,' she suddenly whooped. 'They've taken my dog Fifi! I have just noticed while talking to you. The big pot dog figure of our first dog, Fifi. The most gorgeous, beautiful-natured French poodle you could ever have wished to know. My husband bought it for me . . . as a remembrance of her. It was almost life-size. It had been in this fireplace thirty years or more.'

'Oh dear. I am so sorry. But, tell me, have you noticed an unfamiliar car or a vehicle of any kind loitering around lately?'

'Didn't see anything. Oh dear. Do you think I will ever see my Fifi again? And my photographs? There are pictures of Ernest and me on our honeymoon in Filey, and my dear father and mother on a boat on Lake Lucerne. Oh dear.'

'Don't touch anything. I'll get someone out to you promptly. And not to worry. We'll do all we can to get your stuff back.'

'Oh, thank you so very much, Inspector. I feel so much better talking to you. You are always so very kind to me.'

Angel had a thought. He knew she had a few pet dogs. Four or five. She was extremely fond of them.

'Not at all. Tell me, Mrs Buller-Price, where were your dogs while you were out?'

'Ah. I always put them together in the barn. They seem to enjoy themselves there. There's much more room for them than in the house.'

'Ah, yes. Well, now, let me say goodbye now, and then I can organize a fingerprint man and whatever else is needed to find your burglar and hopefully recover your property quickly.'

'Oh, thank you. Of course. Of course. Hope to see you yourself sometime very soon.'

'Yes, indeed. I'll be round to see you as soon as I can. And you know you can always phone.'

'Thank you, Inspector. Thank you very much indeed. Goodbye.'

'Goodbye,' he said.

He held onto the handset and pressed down on the cradle. He tapped a single digit number.

The eager young voice of probationer PC Ahaz answered. 'CID office.'

'Ahmed, is DS Gawber in there?'

'Yes, sir.'

'Ask him to come to my office, and bring yourself up here as well, pronto.'

'Right, sir.'

He banged down the phone.

He stood up, clasped his hands behind his back and began to walk up and down the little office. His face looked as grim as a rainy day in a caravan.

There was a knock at the door.

'Come in,' he called.

It was DS Gawber and Ahmed.

He looked at Ahmed and pointed to the Weetabix cardboard box on his desk.

'Take that round to Mr Twelvetrees at the CPS, with my compliments.'

'Right, sir.'

Ahmed picked up the box and went out.

Gawber closed the door after him, then came up to the desk.

Angel said, 'You remember Mrs Buller-Price up at Tunistone?'

'Yes, of course.'

'She was burgled yesterday afternoon. Thief took mostly very nice pieces. In broad daylight. Nice-looking house in the middle of nowhere. Got in by a downstairs window. Minimal disturbance. No vehicle seen. Nothing seen. Who does that make you think of?'

Gawber frowned for a moment then looked at Angel knowingly.

'Harry Hull.'

Angel nodded in agreement.

'Is he out of Armley, yct?'

'I'll find out, sir.'

'Talk to the probation office. They'll have an address for him. And if he hasn't a proper alibi, shake his place down thoroughly. He's as sly as a fox. Once hid a solid gold cigarette case under his next-door neighbour's baby. And go and see Mrs Buller-Price. Find out all you can. And get a fingerprint man up there, and be as quick as you can.'

'Right, sir,' Gawber said, and made for the door.

'And he'd need transport. You'll need to find how he got the stuff away.'

'In his pockets, I expect.'

'No. He also took a pot dog. A poodle. White. Called Fifi.'

Gawber blinked.

'How big?'

'She said life-size.'

'What would it weigh, sir?'

'I don't know,' he said tetchily. 'But more than he'd want to carry back to Bromersley under his arm, I expect.'

Gawber nodded.

The phone rang.

Angel glanced at it and then back at Gawber.

'Well, crack on with it, Ron,' he said impatiently.

Gawber nodded and went out.

Angel picked up the receiver.

It was Detective Superintendent Harker.

'Yes, sir?'

'A body has been pulled out of the River Don under Town End Bridge,' he growled. 'SOCO's been told. Get on to it. And don't make a meal out of it. I've enough on with this H business. Uniformed has responded to a triple nine; John Weightman's down there dealing with it.'

There was a click and the phone went dead.

* * *

Angel saw a plain white van he recognized as SOCO's, behind a Leeds Police Sub Aqua Squad 4 x 4 Range Rover, parked on Town End Bridge, a busy road over the River Don in the centre of Bromersley. Around forty people, some with bulging shopping bags, had congregated on the bridge and were peering over the wall at the activity below. He drove his BMW up to a few yards behind the white transit and parked. He stepped lively to the top of the steps that led down to the flagstone path running alongside the bank of the river. As he hurried down he saw four men in white paper suits hastily draping a small framework of plastic scaffolding with white sheeting to provide concealment around a body, which was on the path covered with a plastic sheet. At the bottom of the steps, big John Weightman was unrolling blue and white 'POLICE DO NOT CROSS' tape across them. He saw Angel approaching and lifted the tape to let him through.

'Ta. Now then, John. Everything all right?'

Weightman saluted and said, 'Good morning, sir. Yes.' He nodded towards the activity a few yards beyond and pulled a face. 'Nasty mess they've made of him.'

Angel frowned and continued towards the scene of crime. A frogman leapt out of the water and began to undo the straps on his oxygen tank, while another man in a wet suit began unfastening a rope from around his waist.

SOCO's DS Taylor in whites, mask and rubber boots saw Angel approaching and came across to meet him.

'Good morning, sir.'

Angel nodded.

'Now, Don, what you got?'

Taylor pulled the mask down away from his mouth. 'Young woman made a triple nine call, reported a body in the river at 8.50 this morning. John Weightman was first here. He called the Leeds Police Sub Aqua Squad out. They pulled a man's body out just under the bridge there,' he said, pointing to the middle of the river almost directly under the bridge. 'They brought him over to the bank. And left him here. A quick look at him showed that he'd been shot once in the chest and has some injury to his left hand.'

'Any ID?'

'Not yet, sir. Haven't searched him. Wanted to get him out of the gaze of everybody.'

Angel agreed and nodded.

'He looks about sixty or seventy, though, well dressed, grey hair.'

Angel rubbed his chin. He couldn't recall anybody in that age group having been reported missing over the past few days.

'Have a look as soon as you can and let me know. Have you advised Dr Mac?'

'He's on his way.'

Angel's mobile began to ring.

He nodded at Taylor, turned away and reached into his pocket.

The sergeant returned to erecting the screen.

Angel pulled out his mobile and pressed the button. It was Harker.

'Have you identified that body yet?' he growled.

'No, sir.'

'Hmm. Joshua Gumme's wife has phoned in to report he's missing. Says he went missing last night. Hasn't been home. She's very worried about him.'

'As soon as I know, sir, I'll ring you back.'

The line went dead.

Angel blinked. He knew Joshua Gumme. Their paths had crossed several times over the years. He had often wondered how on earth that crook had managed to stay out of prison. He had sailed perilously close to it many a time. He owned businesses in Bromersley including a snooker hall. Had a little printing business. Irons in all sorts of pies. Recently had acquired the reputation of being unbeatable at card games, and had the unofficial tag of 'the man who couldn't lose'. Had become immensely wealthy by local standards. Had some sort of an illness that had put him in a wheelchair. His wife, Myra, was dead, he remembered. Knew he'd remarried but didn't know anything about the woman.

He turned back to the scene and went over to the Sub Aqua team. Two men, both still in wet suits, had taken off the flippers, helmets and bottles and were sitting on a grass patch, drinking soup out of flasks.

'I'm DI Angel,' he said. 'Where exactly did you find the body, then?'

'I'm DS Stranger, sir,' one of them replied, pointing a hand across the water. 'Directly under the bridge, about twelve feet from the bank.'

'Is it deep there?'

'No. About eight feet or less.'

Angel nodded. 'It's imperative we find the murder weapon. Look out for a gun of some sort?'

'Yes, of course, sir,' Stranger said as he screwed the lid on his flask. 'We have planned to make a systematic search of an area, stretching from one side of the river to the other, ten feet wide, and in line with where we recovered the body. That should cover the likely area where anything heavy thrown from this side of the bridge might sink. But anything small like that might take some finding even with our detectors. We'd need about a week, sir.'

Angel nodded.

'That should do it.'

'There's a bicycle or a pram stuck down there in mud. Next to where he was. Tried to move it, it's a bit heavy.'

Angel's eyebrows shot up.

'If it's a wheelchair, get it up. It probably belongs to him,' he said, nodding towards the place where the SOCO men were fastening the flapping sheeting to the scaffolding. 'Could be valuable evidence.'

Stranger looked surprised.

'Disabled, was he, sir?'

'Yes. And anything else around there that you think might be pertinent to this case.'

'You're looking for a hard nut, sir,' Stranger said. 'Who would throw a man in a wheelchair off a bridge?'

* * *

'Ahmed, I want you to contact the phone company and get a list of calls made from Mr Gumme's mobile and his home phone, over the past two weeks.'

'Right, sir.'

Angel's phone rang. He reached out for it.

'Angel.'

'This is reception, sir. There's a lady, a Mrs Gumme to see you.'

'Right. I won't keep her a minute. I'm sending PC Ahaz straight up for her.'

'Right, sir.'

He replaced the phone and looked up at Ahmed.

'She's here. Nip off smartly and bring her down.'

Ahmed dashed out of the office and up the corridor.

Two minutes later, he strode down the green corridor followed by a woman taking small rapid steps because of her slim pencil skirt and high-heeled shoes.

Angel was at his office door to greet her.

'Thank you for being so prompt, Mrs Gumme.'

She nodded.

He looked sympathetically into her heavily made-up face. Her eyes were red and her lips trembling. And there was a smell of something sweet and unusual. It must have been perfume.

'Thank you for coming in,' he said, holding out his hand to shake hers. He rubbed his chin with the other. 'I'm so sorry to be the bearer of such sad news.'

'Someone has to . . . *had* to tell me,' she said in a small voice. He noticed that when relaxed her mouth was usually open slightly, and her lips formed the letter O.

'Would you like a cup of tea?' he said.

There was a brief smile. She lowered her thick eyelashes momentarily and nodded.

Angel looked at Ahmed and held up three fingers.

Ahmed understood and rushed down the corridor to the private little cupboard in the CID room.

'If it's all the same to you,' Angel said, putting his hand on her elbow and steering her towards Interview Room 2, 'we'll record this interview. It will avoid going over it twice and save time.'

'I'm all for that, Inspector. I have to get back. There is so much to do.'

She sighed. The eyelashes dropped then flickered up.

'Oh dear. Now that Joshua is . . . dead, I have to do everything myself.' She dabbed her eyes with a tissue. 'It's something I've got to get used to.'

He pointed to a chair by the table. She sat down quickly and put a small handbag on the table in front of her.

Angel looked at her; he couldn't imagine this woman as an appropriate partner for Joshua Gumme, wheelchair-bound, ill-mannered, card-playing crook.

He pushed a tape into the machine. He checked that the red light was on and the spools turning.

'Tell me about last night.'

'Yes. Hmm. We had dinner at home as usual about seven, the two of us, then at eight Joshua pushed his chair away from the table—'

'Who was in the house at that time?'

'Just Joshua, and me.'

Angel nodded.

'Joshua pushed himself away from the table. He was rather quiet. I knew something was wrong. I had asked him but he wouldn't tell me. I assumed it was to do with the business. It almost always was. He went into the office and made a phone call. Then he came out and said he had to go out and that he'd phoned Horace — that's Horace Makepiece — to come round and collect him. He was Joshua's chauffeur.'

Angel nodded. He'd heard of him. He was known around as Horace 'Harelip' Makepiece. 'So you and your husband were not really on the very best of terms last night, then?'

Her eyes flashed, she rapidly sucked in air and her bosom increased four inches.

'We were fine,' she said. 'Just fine.' Then she pulled her white blouse down an inch at the neckline to show more clearly a necklace comprising twenty or more small carved heart-shaped garnets, each in a delicate old gold setting and connected by pretty leaf motif chain links.

'See that, Inspector whatever-your-name-is? Last night, just before he left, he gave this to me. It's beautiful, ain't it? Antique.'

Angel agreed, but she needn't have made such a performance about it. He wasn't making any particular point. He shrugged.

'Very nice,' he said, to be polite.

She flicked the eyelashes again and smiled.

'So Horace Makepiece came round to the house?' he said, moving on quickly.

'Yes. He was round in a few minutes. Wheeled my husband out to the Bentley . . . and that was the last I saw of him . . .' Her voice trailed away.

'And you had no idea where he was going?'

'Not at the time. When Joshua wasn't back at ten, I began to wonder where he could have gotten to. I tried to get Horace. There was no reply from any of the numbers. I phoned everywhere. Nobody knew anything about either of them. I was beginning to be seriously worried. I thought that even if Joshua had got stuck in a card game somewhere, he would have told Horace to let me know. I went to bed but I couldn't sleep. I got up about two-thirty, went into the sitting room and poured myself a stiff whisky, drank it, came back and eventually dropped off to sleep. I woke up with a start at nine o'clock. It was the doorbell ringing. I was a bit groggy, but I got out of bed, threw on my housecoat and went down to see that it was Horace. He had come to collect my husband. He said he had dropped him off at The Feathers last night and he had told him to leave him there, he'd make his own way home, but to be certain to pick him up here at nine this morning. I told him my husband hadn't been back all night and that I didn't know where he was. I asked him why I couldn't reach him on his mobile last night and he simply said that he had switched it off. He looked really scared, then he said he'd go out and look for him. He knew his haunts, so off he went. I had a quick swim in the pool to clear my head, then a few minutes on the sunbed to think things out, then I phoned the police. The rest you know.'

'Where can I get in touch with Horace Makepiece now?'

'Horace? He normally doesn't go far. If he isn't at his flat, he'll be in the printing shop or at the billiard hall on Duke Street or the bookies next door. I'll give you the numbers. I'll write them down.'

She zipped open the small white leather handbag.

'Got some paper?'

Angel watched her slim, white, manicured fingers fumbling around inside the bag. He reached into the drawer in the table, looking for something for her to write on. He found a pad of Witness Statement forms. He pulled it out, closed the drawer, dropped it on the table and pushed it across in front of her.

She held up a stubby, gold-coloured ballpoint pen she had exhumed from her handbag.

'Ah. Thank you.'

She squared the pad in front of her and began writing.

The door opened and Ahmed came in with the teas. He passed them round as Mrs Gumme was writing. Then he sat down next to Angel.

Angel patiently sipped the tea.

Mrs Gumme finished, looked over her handiwork, nodded and pushed the pad over to Angel.

'There. I have put the addresses *and* the phone numbers of the places where he usually hangs out.'

Angel glanced at it and raised his eyebrows. It was neatly printed in an irregular assortment of block and lower-case letters, and numbers of the same size. Although unusual, it was perfectly clear and understandable.

'Thank you, Mrs Gumme.'

He tore off the page, folded it roughly, slipped it into his inside jacket pocket and put the pad back in the table drawer.

'Tell me, did your husband have any particular enemies who might have wanted him . . . out of the way?'

The eyelashes flickered briefly.

'Joshua was always a winner. He never lost at anything he did. He was bound to upset people . . . he wasn't the most tactful person . . .'

'Was there anybody in particular?'

'He didn't tell me everything. I don't know. There might have been people from the old days.'

'What old days?'

She shook her head. She looked as if she wished she hadn't said that. Now she didn't know what to say.

Angel waited.

She would have to say something. The eyelashes flickered again.

'Before I knew him,' she said. 'Horace would know all about that.'

'I'm asking you, Mrs Gumme.'

'I don't know much about his past. I've known him ten years. He was fifty when I met him. Horace has known him thirty or forty years.'

Angel wasn't happy.

'Mrs Gumme, do you know of anybody who might have murdered your husband?'

'No.'

'You said he had been quiet last night.'

'Over dinner. He was. Yes. But I have no idea what was on his mind.'

Angel rubbed his chin.

'Who would benefit most financially from his death?'

The heavy eyelids flicked open. Her eyes flashed. Her mouth tightened.

'I would, I suppose.'

Angel rubbed his chin.

'Did your husband have any family?'

'A son, Edmund. Lives in York somewhere. Met him once.'

'Only once?'

'The lad took himself away when Joshua's first wife Myra died. Cut Joshua up quite a bit, he used to say, but he got over it. Joshua's not spoken to him . . . they've not spoken to each other in years, as far as I know.'

Angel thought it was sad.

'Do you have a phone number or an address?'

She shook her head. Then she raised her eyelashes and said, 'Tell you who will know. Carl Messenger. That's Joshua's solicitor.'

Angel nodded. Then he nodded again. Slightly more energetically. He had heard of Messenger. He was thinking how appropriate it was for a slightly dodgy businessman to have a slightly dodgy solicitor.

'One last question for now, Mrs Gumme.'

She looked up. She looked pleased and licked her dry lips. 'Yeah. Sure.'

'Did your husband own a gun?'

She hesitated.

'Yes. I believe he did.'

Angel thought this a strange reply.

'Either he did or he didn't,' he said evenly.

'Yes, he did, Inspector.'

'What make was it?'

'It was a Walther PPK/S .32 automatic. German.'

'Where does he keep it?'

'In his desk drawer. He used to carry it . . . sometimes.'

'Did he have a licence for it?' He knew he wouldn't have.

'I dunno.'

'What did he want it for?'

'What does anybody carry a gun for? He was a rich man . . . stuck in a chair. He was always careful. Didn't want to be at a disadvantage.'

'Was he carrying it last night?'

He noticed her hands were trembling.

'Must have been. When he didn't come home that was one of the first places I looked. I knew if the Walther wasn't there, he'd have been expecting trouble and he would have taken it with him. And that's when I really began to be frightened.'

THREE

It was 8.28 a.m. when Angel arrived at his office. He was taking off his coat when Ahmed peered through the open door.

'Good morning, sir.'

'Come in if you're coming,' Angel said impatiently. There was a lot to do. He had a murderer to catch.

Ahmed was carrying a newspaper.

'Have you seen this, sir?' he said as he closed the door. 'It's about this Joshua Gumme murder.'

He pushed the newspaper in front of him.

Angel picked it up. It was the *South Yorkshire Daily Times*. Ahmed pointed to the bottom of the front page.

There was a photograph of Gumme in his wheelchair, smiling benignly. Under the photograph it read:

MAN WHO COULDN'T LOSE MURDERED!
GUMME THE GAMBLER DEAD
The brutally assaulted body of Joshua Gumme, 60, was
dragged out of the River Don under Town End Bridge,

Bromersley, on Wednesday morning. He had suffered a gun-shot wound.

Gumme, who rose to the top of the card-playing world, once washed cars in the streets for shoppers at ten pence a car. He died one of the richest men in Bromersley, having various business interests in the town, including owning and operating the snooker hall on Duke Street.

Dubbed 'the man who couldn't lose' by the British Pontoon Club because he played over 200 games of pontoon without losing a single one, judges and experts were called in to supervise Gumme closely at the table. Since his lucky streak began, ten years ago, in 1997, his person, clothes, the table and cards have been examined by every kind of expert several times and nothing dishonest was ever found. When our reporter asked him to what did he attribute his success, he said, 'I was just born lucky, I expect.'

If there was some system, scheme, ploy or device that assisted Joshua Gumme's amazing and infallible talent, the secret has died with him or is now in the hands of his murderer.

He leaves a widow and a son, Edmund Gumme.

Angel rubbed his chin.

'Thank you, Ahmed,' he said, returning the paper. He leaned forward and dragged that morning's mail towards the centre of the desk.

'Could you play pontoon, sir, and win two hundred games on the trot?'

'No. I couldn't, lad. Nor could anyone else,' Angel said, slipping the blade of a paperknife into an envelope.

'But it says—'

'I know what it says, Ahmed. But you mustn't believe all you read in the papers.'

'No, sir. But how could he possibly win two hundred games, one after the other like that?'

Angel shook his head.

'Because he cheated, that's how. Pontoon is mainly a game of chance, isn't it? The cards wouldn't come out in the favour of anyone two hundred consecutive times, would they?'

Ahmed nodded. He seemed convinced. He made for the door. 'It said that he was very carefully watched by judges and experts, though, sir,' he added.

'Well, don't look at me, Ahmed. I don't know how he did it.'

Ahmed smiled.

'But you'll find out, sir, won't you?'

Angel shrugged and put a letter down on the desk. 'I have a lot more important jobs to do than that,' he said. 'And so have you,' he added quickly. 'Firstly, get me Dr Mac. He'll likely be at the mortuary. Then I want to speak to Don Taylor of SOCOs. Then see if you can find an Edmund Gumme . . . information is that he lives in or near York. You could try the phone book. The electoral roll. Or check him on the PNC. If he hasn't been convicted of an offence, of course, he won't be there. You'll have to do it the hard way.'

The phone rang. He reached out for it.

'Angel.'

It was DC Scrivens.

'Good morning, sir.' He sounded excited about something. 'Just overheard from Traffic that a car was found burning in a field of wheat, off a track, off Wath Lane. It's in the middle of nowhere, sir,' he said excitedly.

Angel growled like a bear.

'I'm not a bloody fireman, Scrivens! What do you want me to do about it?'

Undeterred, Scrivens continued, 'It's Gumme's Bentley, sir! You're on that case, aren't you?'

Angel rubbed his chin. Then he sniffed.

'Had it been reported missing?'

'No, sir. There's about eighty thousand quid's worth there.'

'Yes. Well done, Scrivens. What are you busy with?'

'A shoplifting, sir.'

'Well, put that on hold and follow this up for me. Find out what caused it. Any fingerprints, anything at all. Where was it taken from and how was it done. Have a word with Mrs Gumme. Find out about the car keys. Mileage, all that stuff. Jump on it pronto and let me know.'

'Right, sir,' the young man said excitedly. He preferred working on murder cases to shoplifting any time.

Angel replaced the phone.

That was an utterly confusing piece of news. It was usually much cheaper cars with less security that were stolen for joy-riding, and then driven to some outrageous place to be torched. He had never heard of a Bentley suffering such treatment.

'Ahmed,' Angel began.

The phone rang again. He picked up the receiver. It was the superintendent.

'Come down here. Smartly!' Harker bellowed.

'Right, sir.'

The line went dead. He frowned. Must be something urgent. He put the phone down and crossed to the door.

'Got to go, Ahmed. Better hold off those jobs. But see if you can get that phone number for Edmund Gumme in York.'

'Right, sir.'

Angel made his way sharply down the corridor to the superintendent's office. It sounded urgent. He hoped it wasn't something time-consuming. He had enough on his plate at that moment.

He knocked at the door and pushed it open.

Harker was at his desk. Opposite him were two other men, much younger. One was Sergeant Galbraith of the uniformed branch of Bromersley force who was, of course, known to him. Angel had thought that he was a quiet, thoroughly dependable copper. The other man was in plain clothes; he thought he knew him vaguely.

'Come in,' Harker said. 'Come in. You know DCI Gardiner from the Central Drugs Squad?'

'Good morning, sir,' Angel said. He remembered his face. He had met him once at a drugs briefing in Leeds. He now recalled that he was a live wire and seemed to know the drugs business backwards.

The DCI nodded and smiled politely.

'Sit down. Sit down,' Harker said. 'I really wanted a bigger turn-out than this but everybody else seems to be out of the building or tied up with something.'

Gardiner coughed.

Harker's eyebrows shot up. He glanced at him, wrinkled his nose and said, 'The DCI has something to say.'

'Yes. Thank you, sir,' Gardiner began. 'It is simply that we have intelligence that a local woman is dealing H locally in a big way. For security reasons, I'll keep her name and address schtum, but with the super's permission, I am calling a raid on her house for ten hundred hours. I'd go now, but we've got to have time for the dog handler to get here from Nottingham. I have got Wakefield to send an ARV as a precaution; I don't think she's armed, but you never can tell. All right?'

Angel and Galbraith glanced at each other, then nodded.

'Yes, sir.'

'I'll need, minimally, four officers from this station,' Gardiner continued, 'including at least two women. Will you organize that, Inspector, and assemble in the duty office at 09.55 hours?'

Angel wrinkled his nose.

'Yes, sir.'

* * *

Two unmarked police cars came down Edmondson's Avenue, while the ARV and the dog handler's van came up it. They had been directed to stop at the red letterbox, which was a useful landmark, being directly opposite number twenty-six.

The eight police personnel and the dog piled out of the vehicles and ran up Gloria Swithenbank's garden path. Leading the party were the two men in armoured jackets and helmets from the ARV carrying Heckler and Koch G36C rifles and a battering ram; immediately behind them were DI Angel and WPC Baverstock. They raced past the front window, then round the corner to the back of the house, tried the door, yelled out, 'Police. We're coming in,' and went straight through.

The armed team charged through the empty kitchen into the tiny front room followed by DI Angel and WPC Baverstock and were surprised to find the householder with her mother, calmly drinking tea and watching television. One armed man raced up to the bathroom to stop the lavatory being used to flush drugs away, while the other checked round the house for any solid fuel heater or fire to prevent the disposal of them by incineration.

At the same time, the other four members of the team, DCI Gardiner, Sergeant Galbraith, another WPC and a PC dog handler with an excitable spaniel, who began to bark, took up positions outside the front door of the house, and began a barrage of knocking and yelling, 'Police. Open up. Police. Come on.'

Gloria Swithenbank jumped to her feet. Her mouth tightened; her eyes glowed like two pieces of coke in a furnace.

'Mercy me!' she bawled. 'What do you want?'

'Police,' Angel said, and held up his ID and an A4 sheet of letterhead with typing on it.

'Police? What police? What on earth is happening?'

'Mrs Gloria Swithenbank?' Angel asked.

'Yes. What the hell is going on?'

'I am a police officer. I have a search warrant. How many people are there in the house?'

An elderly lady was sitting on the settee facing the television, her mouth wide open in surprise.

'What is it, Gloria?' she said and began shaking.

Angel called across to her. 'It's all right, love. We're the police.'

'What are you looking for? I haven't committed any crime,' Gloria Swithenbank said.

'How many people are in the house?'

'Just me and my mother. Look, you're frightening her.'

'What's her name?'

'Gladstone. Alice Gladstone.'

Angel called across to her again. 'It's all right, Mrs Gladstone. We're just looking for something.'

He turned to WPC Baverstock and made a signal to go to the old lady and attend to her.

The two men with rifles bustled noisily into the room.

'Every room checked, sir. No attics and no cellars,' one of them said.

Angel nodded.

There was still the racket from outside.

Angel went to the front door. The key was in the door, so he turned it and let DCI Gardiner and the others in. They crowded into the room.

Gloria Swithenbank glared at them.

'What's this all about?'

DCI Gardiner made his way up to her and said, 'You must be Mrs Gloria Swithenbank.'

She turned to him and sniffed. 'What if I am?'

'We have reason to believe that these premises are being used for the illegal distribution of Class A drugs,' he said. 'Do you want to tell me where they are?'

She pulled an astonished face, shook her head, put her hands on her hips and said, 'Don't be ridiculous. I don't know what you're talking about.'

'Very well,' DCI Gardiner said calmly, then he turned to the raiding party and allocated an area of the house and garden to be searched by them. Angel was teamed up with Sergeant Galbraith to search the upstairs two bedrooms, bathroom, landing and staircase.

Angel suggested they start in the bathroom and began to make his way up the stairs followed by WPC Baverstock and the other WPC, who were escorting a protesting Gloria Swithenbank and her mother to a bedroom for a body search.

Angel found himself on the bathroom floor, where he unscrewed the chromium-topped screws that were holding the plastic boxing round the underside of the bath. He took the boards away; all he found was dust and fluff.

The dog handler had let his excited spaniel off the lead and given him the run of the house, carefully following him round. The dog rushed into the bathroom, looked round it, wagged its tail, sniffed along the carpet down the side of the bath then looked away, disinterested. The handler pointed under the washbasin. The dog went under it, sniffed, wagged its tail and came straight out.

Galbraith removed a mirror over the bathroom sink, found nothing and screwed it back. Angel and Galbraith together pulled up fitted carpets to see if any floorboards were loose or had been recently disturbed, looked for any fresh sawing or cutting marks and turned the pictures on the walls to see if there was any hiding place behind them. They searched thoroughly the beds, the wardrobes, the cupboards and the drawers. They even checked for any hollow-sounding places in the walls. The stairs were just as carefully scrutinized for loose floorboards. In fact, they looked every possible place where drugs or a stash of cash could be concealed. Nothing.

Angel knew that downstairs the team would be just as thorough, and that they would examine every package containing foodstuffs in the kitchen cupboard as well as everything in the refrigerator and deep freeze.

After two hours, Angel and Galbraith went down the stairs to the sitting room. He saw the DCI was still interviewing Mrs Swithenbank and her mother. By the look on his face he might just as well have been talking to Mrs Buller-Price's pot poodle Fifi.

With a nod from the DCI, Angel and the rest of the team packed up their traps and left the house almost as quickly as they had arrived. The raid had obviously not provided sufficient evidence for a charge. They gathered outside in the street.

'Well, thank you, everybody,' Gardiner said. 'You'd better return to your own respective offices. I regret the waste of time. This tip-off was, regrettably, a turkey.'

The dog handler said, 'Sir. The dog did react positively at a cupboard in the kitchen. I pulled everything out and let him have a good old sniff around, but there was nothing to be found. It was spotlessly clean. Also on the kitchen table. Even though it would have been wiped down, even scrubbed, the dog did detect the recent presence of a Class A drug on the top. Perhaps it had been used in the preparing of twists or packets.'

The DCI looked skywards and ran his hand through his hair.

'Can you rely on that dog?'

'Absolutely, sir.'

He rubbed his hand across his mouth.

'Who checked the vacuum cleaner?'

WPC Baverstock put up a hand.

'I did, sir. There was hardly anything in it. The bag must have been changed recently. I emptied it out on a sheet of newspaper. There were no signs of H or any other illegal substance.'

'Did the dog sniff it?'

'Yes, sir. But there was nothing. I also checked the carpet sweeper, and got the same result.'

'Did anybody find *anything* . . . *anything* else at all unusual in the house . . . or garden?'

Nobody said anything.

Gardiner threw up his arms.

'Right. Thank you, everybody. Let's go.'

He leaned forward to get into the car.

Angel called out, 'She was tipped off, sir.'

The DCI's head shot back out.

* * *

'I've got more to do with my time than oversee time-wasting raids on old biddies scratching out an existence on a council estate,' Harker said with a sniff. He was drumming his fingers on his desk while licking his lips and shaking his head.

Angel looked down at him. He was uglier than usual. He'd seen better-looking orang-utans — and his moustache could do with trimming. He recalled that he'd started growing it that way about the same time the postman had delivered a book addressed to him at the police station in a cellophane cover called *The Love Life of Josef Stalin*.

'It wasn't like that, sir,' Angel said.

'The DCI says the intelligence was rubbish.'

'I don't think it was, sir. When we arrived, everything was just too perfect. It was ten o'clock in the morning. The beds were made. There were no pots in the sink. All signs of a meal had been cleared away. Everywhere had been vacuumed and tidied round, just as if they had been expecting visitors. Also, neither of the women worked; Gloria Swithenbank said they had no savings and no debts, therefore we are expected to believe that they survived solely on her mother's pension. The rent is eighty-four quid a week. Swithenbank had sixty quid in her purse, her mother had twenty and there was not another bean in the house. The larder was well stocked and she had two bottles of vodka and a hundred cigarettes in the cupboard. It just doesn't add up.'

Harker pursed his lips, then said, 'Perhaps she's on the game?'

Angel smiled. 'Have you seen her?'

He shook his head.

'No, sir,' Angel continued. 'Gloria Swithenbank had been tipped off. And she'd had time to get the drugs and money hidden, where we couldn't find them, get the house straight, make herself presentable and then get her and her mother positioned in front of the telly like two spiced pussies waiting for a knock on the door.'

Harker wrinkled his nose.

'I don't know,' he said, shaking his head.

'Where could the woman hide the stuff so quickly and thoroughly?'

Harker persistently shook his head.

Angel said, 'The dog handler said his dog reacted positively at two places in the kitchen.'

'Really? But then again, could we really put our trust in a dog?'

Angel grabbed the advantage.

'Would you rather put your trust in a man, sir?'

Harker frowned.

'What man?'

'Any man, sir. Say a professional man. Say a doctor?'

'A doctor?' he said grandly. 'Well, yes. Of course, a doctor would be ideal.'

'Such as Harold Shipman.'

Harker's eyes flashed. 'I didn't mean a villain!'

Angel was dead serious.

'There's no deceit in a dog, sir. A dog isn't a villain. It isn't dishonest. It hasn't a record. All it has to hide is bones.'

FOUR

'Come in, Ron,' Angel said, pointing to the chair. 'What did you make of it?'

'Harry Hull was released four weeks ago from Armley,' Gawber said, closing the door.

Angel's eyes lit up.

'Been over his pad?'

'Yes, a little two-room flat, part of a big house, number 101, on Earl Street, but there was nothing of Mrs Buller-Price's there. Or anything else he shouldn't have. He's getting very clever is our Harry.'

'Did he have an alibi?'

'No, sir. Says he was in the flat the whole time. No money to go out and enjoy himself, he says. Can't prove it though.'

'Useless, then. I still reckon it'll be him.'

Angel rubbed his chin slowly, then added, 'And how was Mrs Buller-Price, then?'

'You *know* her, sir. Cheerful and resilient, even though she's had some very choice pieces stolen. Optimistic, too. She expects us to recover them.'

Angel sighed. 'You made a list?'

Gawber dug into his inside pocket, pulled out a folded sheet of A4 and handed it to him.

Angel quickly scanned the list, which comprised £200 in £20 notes, two emerald and diamond rings, a pearl choker, fourteen small silver items including picture frames, and a sixteen-inch tall white pot figure of a French poodle.

Gawber said, 'I don't understand why anyone would steal a pot poodle of that size . . . or any size for that matter. I mean, it wasn't valuable. It wasn't antique. It would be heavy, awkward to carry and difficult to fence.'

Angel nodded.

'A fence would want to charge him rent for taking it in,' he said wryly.

'Does Harry Hull like dogs?' Gawber asked.

'The only thing Harry Hull likes apart from money, booze and women is Harry Hull. I've got another idea. Nip down to Dolly Reuben's. See if she's got a white pot dog for sale.'

Dolly Reuben ran a tatty second-hand furniture shop on Cemetery Road. It had been the front for her husband's business. Frank Reuben was the biggest fence in South Yorkshire, until he was caught in possession of £4,000 worth of newly minted 20p pieces stolen from a security van in transit between South Wales and London. Frank was in the middle of a five-year stretch in Pentonville.

'Right, sir,' said Gawber.

'Take a sneaky look through her shop window, before you go in.'

Gawber smiled, nodded and made for the door.

'And on your way out, tell Ahmed I want him.'

'Right, sir.'

The door closed.

Angel sighed, scratched his head and leaned back in the swivel chair. He really must get on with investigating Joshua Gumme's murder. His next of kin must be informed. Everything else must wait. He would have to delegate more.

There was a knock on the door.

'Come in.'

It was PC Ahaz flourishing a piece of paper.

'I didn't know you were back, sir. I've got Edmund Gumme's address and telephone number,' he said, putting the paper on his desk.

'Right, Ahmed. Ta. Now, what's DS Crisp doing?'

'Don't know, sir. I haven't seen him this morning.'

Angel glanced at the note in front of him, picked up the phone and began tapping in the number.

'Well, see if you can *find* him and tell him I want him. SAP.'

'Right, sir,' Ahmed said as he closed the door.

'I'll have to put a collar and lead on that lad,' he muttered.

He still had the phone against his ear and was listening to the ringing-out tone. It suddenly clicked and a recorded man's voice said, 'This is Edmund Gumme. I regret I am not able to take your call. Please leave a message and your number and I'll get back to you.'

Angel hesitated. He didn't want to leave a recorded message telling him his father had been shot dead and dumped in a river. He put his hand on the cradle and ended the call. Then he tapped in another number. It was ringing out.

There was a knock at the door.

'Come in,' he called.

The door opened. It was DS Crisp.

'You wanted me, sir?'

Angel's eyebrows shot up. His lips tightened across his teeth. He banged the telephone down in its cradle.

'Come in, Sergeant. I was just ringing you on your mobile. Where have you been? You're supposed to be on my team yet I can never get hold of you.'

DS Crisp's mouth dropped open.

'I'm sorry, sir. I've been very busy. Maybe my mobile's faulty again. You had told me to deal with that attack on that postman?'

'That was ages ago.'

'It was Tuesday before I got to it, sir. The day before yesterday.'

'Well, it was only an hour's job, wasn't it?'

'The man was hurt, sir. Had to go to hospital,' he said pointedly.

Angel knew already that he was losing the argument. He indicated the chair.

'Tell me about it,' he said patiently.

'Right, sir. Yes. A fifty-eight-year-old postman was in a post office van returning from collecting post from letter-boxes in the outlying villages west of Bromersley . . . Tunistone, Gullbush, Hoylandswaine . . . round there. It was about seven o'clock Monday evening when he reached his last pick-up point, which was a box in the wall, next to the Frog's Leap Inn at Midspring. He stopped and while he was filling the sack, somebody hit him on the back of the neck with something hard and he fell on the pavement. When he woke up, he was on a trolley in A and E in the Bromersley General.'

'Was he badly hurt?'

'Nasty bump on his head. He was off work three days.'

'What was taken?'

'Nothing. The van was not touched, and the post seemed all right. There was a bit of a panic when the manager couldn't find the postman's keys, but the next day they turned up in the gutter not far from where he fell.'

Angel ran his hand across his mouth.

'So what did you do?'

'Nothing more I could do. The man could have died.'

'Yes, but he didn't. Have you any witnesses? Any forensic? Is the postman known to us? What's the motive?'

Crisp's mouth dropped open.

Then he said, 'No witnesses, sir. No forensic. The man is not known to us. I don't know what the motive was. Kids trying their arm, I expect, then getting scared and running off.'

Sticking his jaw out, he shook his head and said, 'Is there anything more you can do to find out who attacked this poor chap?'

'No, sir.'

'Right,' he snapped. 'Well, let's move on. Push off and file your report while it's fresh, then come back here. I've an urgent job for you. It should have been done yesterday. I want you to go to York to find a man.'

* * *

Angel managed to clear some of the paperwork off his desk and then strolled down the corridor, out of the rear door to the station vehicle park. He got into his car and drove it to The Fat Duck for a change of scene. It was only a three-minute trip from his office and was his favourite pub. He hoped he might bump into a snout he knew, who might have been able to supply him with a tasty morsel of underworld gossip. He would have particularly liked any information about Joshua Gumme and his recent activities. In any event, the informant didn't show. He met several familiar friendly faces, exchanged a few courtesies and indulged in a pint of Old Peculier, a meat pie and several slices of black pudding stabbed conveniently with cocktail sticks offered on the bar.

Through the friendly chatter, mostly about football, he heard a phone ring. It was his mobile. He dived into his pocket, turned away from the bar and the noise and made towards the door. He pressed the button and checked the LCD screen.

It was Harker.

Angel blinked. It wasn't usual for the superintendent to contact him on his mobile. He wondered what was wrong.

He quickly pressed the speak button.

'Angel here. Yes, sir?'

'Another post office van driver attacked,' Harker bawled, 'while emptying a postbox on Earl Street! His van stolen. Uniformed are there. I've sent Crisp, but I want you in on it. It's getting very worrying.'

'Right, sir.'

Angel agreed, physical attacks in daylight hours were always extremely worrying.

He closed up the mobile, emptied his glass, ran out of The Fat Duck, got into his car, pulled out of the car park, turned left into Sheffield Road, then left again into Earl Street. Apart from a dress shop on the corner, Earl Street consisted entirely of houses, mostly terraced.

He couldn't see any signs of police vehicles, or a postbox. He changed up to top gear and put his foot down on the accelerator. The long street had a dog's leg bend towards the bottom of it. He followed it round to reveal an ambulance, a marked police Range Rover and Crisp's car parked at the side of the road, one behind the other. Fifteen people were clustered around something on the pavement. He sped up to the scene, stopped and got out of the car. He could hear Crisp despatching six PCs on a house-to-house enquiry. Big

PC John Weightman was waving his arms expansively and saying, 'Did anybody see what happened? Come along now, if you didn't see the assault, please move along. Thank you. Did you see anything, sir?'

Angel forced his way through the crowd.

'Police, excuse me, sir, madam. Please let me pass. Thank you.'

He reached the centre of the throng and could now see two medics, one in blue and one in predominately white, crouched over the still figure of a middle-aged man on the pavement, fixing a collar block round his neck, a stretcher by his side, and behind them a letterbox with its door wide open, half filled with post and a few envelopes scattered on the pavement.

Crisp spotted his boss and made his way across to him. Angel saw him.

'Ah, Crisp. What happened? Anybody see what happened?'

'No, sir. Looks like while the postman was emptying the letterbox, somebody assaulted him and stole his van.'

'Have you its number?'

'No. I've got Scrivens trying to find out from the GPO.'

Angel grunted and leaned over the medics and said, 'I'm DI Angel. How is he?'

'Very weak pulse. Shallow breathing. Unconscious.'

Angel's lips tightened against his teeth.

Then the medic said, 'Got to get him to hospital.'

'Yes,' Angel agreed determinedly.

The two ambulance men started to drag the injured man onto the stretcher.

Angel straightened up and came face to face with big PC John Weightman.

'Sir?' Weightman said.

'Ah, John. Help get this injured man to hospital, smartly. He's in a bad way. Go with him. Try to get a description of his assailant. And what happened.'

'Right, sir,' he said, and he opened his great arms to the small crowd and said, 'There's a man seriously injured here. Make way, please. Make way. Thank you.'

Angel turned to Crisp.

'Send someone to the hospital to take over from John Weightman at the end of his shift. He might have come round by then.'

Crisp nodded.

Angel continued, 'Any idea what the assailant looked like?'

'Nobody saw anything, sir. Hoping to learn something from the house to house.'

A siren began blaring out. The ambulance zoomed off faster than John Prescott to complimentary canapés.

'Any sign of a weapon?'

'No.'

'I want that van finding. Then I want SOCO to go over it with a fine-tooth comb. I want to find out what the assailant took. Go into the background of the victim. See if he's clean. There's no point in going through the letters left here. The assailant has presumably taken what he wanted, either out of this box or from the mailbags on the stolen van. There may have been registered packets collected from post offices on his round, with money or jewellery or whatever inside. Check on that. And see how this assault relates to that assault on a post-man at Frog's Leap Inn at Midspring on Monday evening.'

'The same MO, sir,' Crisp said enthusiastically. 'Assaulted while he was filling the sack.'

'Yes, except that this time the van was taken,' Angel said. 'Is the thief getting bolder? Well, let's hope you can dig something out. I have to get back. Leave it to you. Let me know how it goes.'

* * *

It was 7.55 p.m. Thursday when Angel arrived at Carl Messenger's office. It was the earliest time he could get to see the man. He knocked and walked into the office-cum-waiting room and closed the door. It was very quiet. The only sign of human existence was the strip light blinking at him from the ceiling.

From an open door, a man's dreamy voice called out, 'Come along in, Inspector. I am ready for you.'

He crossed the room and peered into the gloomy room. All he could see was a copper lampshade beaming light onto a desk. There was no sign of life in the little room. He pushed the door further open to reveal a small, hunched man standing there clutching a big brown envelope. He shuffled forward.

'Pleased to meet you, Inspector,' he said in a slow, breathy voice. 'I am Carl Messenger.'

He held out a small, cold hand.

Angel shook it. It was an unusual experience. He could recall corpses that had been warmer and more animated.

Carl Messenger moved very slowly behind his desk to a chair and slumped into it clumsily.

'Please sit down.'

'Thank you,' Angel said. 'And thank you for seeing me at this late hour.'

'No matter. Like you, I sometimes have to work after hours. Anyway, I dug out the document to which you referred. I must say, I was very sad to hear of the murder of Mr Gumme. And he was such a nice gentleman.'

Angel pursed his lips and frowned. He wondered what planet this man had been living on the past few years. He didn't reply. He looked across the desk at him.

Carl Messenger's eyes were half closed most of the time as if he was drugged or tired, and when he did occasionally open them, he looked in pain. He moved only when absolutely necessary and then very slowly.

He shook the brown envelope and a folded document typed on heavy-duty paper dropped out on the desk. He unfolded it.

'And you are the officer in charge of the investigation?'

Angel nodded and said, 'Have you any notion as to who would want Joshua Gumme dead?'

'Goodness me, no, Inspector. He was sometimes impatient, irritable, abrupt even. But I cannot imagine any circumstances that would ever have justified him being murdered.'

Angel sighed.

'Somebody did.'

'Quite so. Quite so. Now, you wanted to know the beneficiaries?'

'When was the will drawn up?'

'June 2005. It was a very hot day, I remember. I can still see Mr Gumme being wheeled in here to sign it. Remarkable man. He was perspiring and grumbling about the heat, I recall. He was being pushed around, by his very attentive chauffeur.'

Messenger opened the document and peered closely at it.

'Hmmm. Yes,' he mumbled.

Angel rubbed his chin and looked round the little room at the shadows on the walls cast by the desk light.

'Yes. Here it is,' Messenger said. 'He left the house and contents, worth at that time around a million, and an annuity of thirty thousand, and the snooker hall and the printing business, at that date, valued at an estimated two million, also to his wife, Ingrid; and he left a package, a small package, at that date value estimated at six pounds to his son, Edmund.'

Angel frowned.

'Six pounds, did you say, Mr Messenger?'

He nodded.

'I have the package in our strong room. Regrettably, Inspector Angel, it has to be given to Mr Edmund personally, in front of two witnesses who will have to attest to it.'

Angel frowned.

'No other bequests?'

'No, Inspector.'

He sniffed.

'And what was the estimated total value of his estate?'

'On that date, well over three million pounds.'

Angel let out a silent whistle and rubbed the lobe of his ear between finger and thumb. His eyes glazed over.

'I understand,' Messenger said, 'that the majority of the estate comprises a town centre property on Duke Street including a snooker hall, a printers, laundry, restaurant and a block of eight flats. Property prices have increased greatly over the past few years. That figure might be a lot more. But against that, there is inheritance tax mostly at forty per cent . . .'

Angel didn't hear him. The solicitor could have saved his breath. He might just as well have been talking to a pet poodle called Fifi. Angel was still wondering what sort of a man would leave his son six pounds out of an estate over three million.

FIVE

The phone was answered, there was a click and a voice said: 'Mortuary. Good morning. Who is calling?'

'DI Angel. Can I speak to Dr Mac?'

'Hold on, please.'

'Right, thank you,' Angel said, then he hunched up a shoulder to hold the phone to his ear while he reached out to get a note pad from a desk drawer. He rummaged in his pocket for a pen, then took a sip of his tea. He heard the unmistakable clearing of the throat of the Glaswegian, so hastily returned the cup to the saucer with a clatter.

'Good morning, Michael. What's the matter wi' ye? It's not eight-thirty yet. Can't you sleep?'

'You're not very charming this morning, Mac. Sorry if somebody has been eating your porridge, but I've a helluva lot on.'

'You're not on your own, Michael. So have I. We are rushed off our feet here. The throughput here is getting like Smithfields. Now what can I do for ye?'

'Have SOCO delivered a body to you, a Joshua Gumme?'

'Yes. Yes. I've done him. Report coming through by email. You'll get it this afternoon.'

'I'm not asking for the full SP now, Mac, but just need to know a couple of things.'

'Yeah? What?'

'What killed him?'

'A bullet straight through the heart. Looks like a .32.'

'Could it have been a Walther PPK/S .32 automatic?'

'Certainly could have been.'

'From what distance?'

'Hard to say. Could have been very close. Some powder has most likely been disturbed. The tide will have swilled some of the powder away. The River Don is no respecter of crime scenes, you know.'

'Ta. And did Gumme have any other injuries?'

'No.'

Angel sensed that Mac's patience was running out.

'Right, Mac. Thanks very much. Goodbye.'

'Goodbye.'

He replaced the phone and rubbed his chin.

He knew he would get all the details later that day, but the profile of the murderer was taking shape. He nodded with satisfaction, and reached out again for the phone and tapped in a number.

A familiar voice answered, 'SOCO. DS Taylor.'

'Good morning, Don. Michael Angel. That man you pulled out of the Don on Wednesday, Joshua Gumme . . .'

'Yes, sir.'

'Did he have a weapon on him? A gun, a knife?'

'No, sir.'

'No gun? The Leeds underwater team *did* have a good look round?'

'They were searching for the rest of the day. They pulled out his wheelchair . . . we have it here. Seems to be in good nick. Not damaged at all.'

'But nothing else, eh?'

'No, sir.'

'Right, Don. Ta.'

'You'll get our report and his personal effects first thing Monday morning, sir.'

'Right, Don, goodbye.'

* * *

The town hall clock struck ten as Angel turned his BMW into Duke Street and parked it in the only available space in front of Baileys the bookies. A neon sign flashed the word 'Snooker' alternately in red and yellow over a narrow ginnel between the bookies and the Bromersley Building Society. Angel locked the car and walked purposefully under the sign and down the ginnel to the end of the iron railings then turned right and through the open door into a big dusty hall packed out with thirty-six snooker tables with overpowering light units covered by big lampshades suspended over them. It was early, so there weren't many customers; eight young men were standing round holding cues, drinking lager and occasionally sticking their backsides in the air as they attempted to pot a ball.

There was a drinks and sandwich bar on a raised dais located in the middle of the room, and a skinny man with a trilby hat and a harelip was hanging over the serving side of it. He was talking to a huge man with long hair, wearing a check suit. He was standing next to a mop bucket with his hands resting on the handle of a mop. An unopened can of Grolsch was sticking out of his pocket. They saw Angel approaching.

They stopped talking to each other. The skinny man nodded towards Angel in acknowledgement.

'Take over, Bozo,' he said to the big man, then he came quickly round from behind, stepped off the dais and rushed up to Angel's side.

'I'm Horace Makepiece,' he whispered. 'You the copper that phoned?'

Angel nodded. 'Can we go somewhere . . . private?' he said.

Makepiece swivelled his skinny neck around the place.

'Yeah. Sure. I'd rather it was that way.'

He waved a finger to Angel to follow him, and they moved quickly between snooker tables still covered with grey linen sheeting to the far end of the hall, where there were two doors in the wall. One had the word 'Private' marked on it and a simple Yale lock to secure it. Makepiece produced a bunch of keys on a chain fastened to his braces, selected a key and unlocked the door. Then he pressed the switch by the door, and a bright light suspended from the ceiling illuminated the room.

At first sight, Angel thought it was a storeroom. It was dark and smelled of wet clothes that had been dried. Parts of damaged snooker tables leaned against the wall. Packs of snooker cues were piled against boxes of chalk. A wheelchair stood significantly in the corner. There was a large square sink with a draining board. Next to it was a long table covered with a linen sheet draped over the items on it like a contoured model of the Alps not succeeding to conceal a makeshift bar. In the centre of the room was a large circular table with six chairs round it.

He held his hand out grandly towards it.

'OK?'

Angel nodded and pulled out the chair facing the door.

Makepiece sat opposite him.

'We call this the back office. To tell the trute, we ain't got no front office.'

Angel pulled out an envelope from his inside pocket and clicked his pen.

'Now, you're Horace Makepiece?' He didn't mention that he knew his nickname was 'Harelip'.

Makepiece pushed the trilby to the back of his bony head, put his hands on the table and said, 'It'll be about the boss. Isn't it? It's scary, very scary. I know I should've stayed wid him, but I didn't know anything bad was going to happen, did I? And he kept telling me to leave him and go home. And he don't like being argued wid, especially in front of people, you know. He'd get all het up and nasty. So I said, "OK, if you're sure." He swore at me, so I got in the car and brought it back and that's all I knew, until I went to the house in the morning. He'd said to pick him up at nine o'clock. But he wasn't there. Hadn't been home. Ingrid . . . Mrs Gumme was chewing the rag and getting onto me. I told her. She didn't want to know. She kept onto me. It wasn't my fault! I kept telling her. She's afraid too, you see, Inspector. They might be back. To tell the trute, Inspector, I ain't feeling so brave myself.'

Angel sighed.

'Better start at the beginning, Mr Makepiece. Who might be back?'

'Yeah. Sure. Well, this was Tuesday, about eight o'clock. I was doing some printing in the print shop next door. It's chiefly for all the stuff we use in the hall, games match lists and stuff. This was some menus for the Chinese restaurant opposite. I also do letterheads by direct mail. Advertise in magazines. Anyway, the boss phones and says I've to take him to The Feathers straight away. So I switched everything off, locked up, told Bozo, on the way through, that I had to go out for a few minutes.'

Angel was listening and making notes on the back of the envelope in very small writing. Names, he liked to print out.

'Who is Bozo and how do you spell it?' he said craftily.

'Bozo Johnson. I don't know. I don't go for spellin' much. Everybody knows Bozo. That big chap. I was talking to him when you came in. He was just going to do the latrines. He's my number one. Looks after the place when I'm not here. Yes. Mmm. I expect I'll have to make him manager now that . . .'

He raised his eyebrows, rubbed non-existent dust off the top of the table with the palms of his hands and shook his head. He sighed and looked across the table at Angel.

'You know, I never thought we'd lose the boss, Inspector. Not like that.'

'No,' Angel said quietly.

There was a moment's quiet.

Angel waited.

'You'll be looking it up, so I may as well tell you,' Makepiece said. 'Bozo Johnson has served time in Durham for manslaughter. Bozo is short for Benjamin, he was named after some guy that wrote a book what made him famous, but that was years ago. Now Bozo has a bit of bad luck. He gets into an argument with a punter, who reckons he's got hiccups and makes a noise to put him off every time he goes for a black. Now there's a twenty on it, so it's serious. Bozo asks him to be quiet . . . time after time. At least six times. The punter says he ain't doing nothing. Bozo bawls him out. The punter gets rattled and belts him one. Bozo pushes him away. He falls over a bar stool and hits his head on a set of wheels they use for moving barrels and crates. He's rushed to hospital and dies next day. Bozo gets tried for manslaughter. He gets twelve years. But he's out in four because he behaves himself. When he comes out of prison, nobody would look at him. He couldn't get a job anywhere. So the boss gives him this new name, Bozo, and sets him on here to help me. He's only a caretaker really, but the boss reckoned it would make him feel good if we called him "the assistant manager". That's all right by me. He does all the dirty jobs that I used to do. He keeps the place clean and tidy, and the washrooms straight. They're always clean and there's always paper in the lavs, soap in the dispenser and paper towels in the box. He does a good job for me. He's no trouble.'

Angel stifled a smile. That wasn't how he remembered the Ben Johnson case, but he let it go.

'Did you pick Mr Gumme up at his home, then?'

'Yeah. A few minutes past eight, it would be. He was ready waiting for me. Ingrid wasn't pleased about it. Yap, yap, yap. But it had nothing to do with me. The boss wanted to go. That's all I needed to know. I got him there in no time. It's only a mile, I guess. I got his chair out. He said to leave him there and go. Pick him up at home in the morning at nine o'clock. I wheeled him . . . well, no, he pulled away from me. He wheeled himself up to the reception desk. I watched him. He waved me away . . . impatient, like. I came back. Put the car in the garage, as quiet as I could. Didn't want to disturb Ingrid . . . Mrs Gumme. Walked here. Went back to the snooker hall, into the print shop, finished off Mr Wong's new menus. Helped Bozo to finish off the evening, lock up, banked the money in the night safe and went home.'

'At The Feathers, did you see who he was going to meet?'

Makepiece said, 'No. And it's maybe a good job too.'

Angel frowned. 'Why do you say that?'

Makepiece breathed out a length of air and shook his head at the same time.

'It was a contract job, wasn't it? Whoever shot the boss was a professional.'

Angel noticed Makepiece's left hand shaking very slightly.

'They don't leave witnesses,' he continued. 'If I had seen him, and he *knew* I'd seen him, I would be dead now.'

Angel ran the tip of his tongue along his bottom lip.

Makepiece's eyes suddenly lit up.

'Hey. I just thought. Maybe the boss has saved my life. Maybe he didn't want me to see whoever he was going to meet for that very reason!'

He smiled as he thought more about it.

Angel frowned. He wasn't sure the reasoning was good logic.

'Who would want to kill Mr Gumme? You said they might be back? Who did you mean? Someone from the old days? Mrs Gumme thought that it could have been someone from the old days. Who was she referring to?'

Makepiece's face assumed a frightened rabbit look. He shrugged and looked away.

'I dunno, do I?'

'You've known him a long time. Twenty years? Thirty years?'

'More than thirty.'

Makepiece shrugged again. He took his hat off, ran his hand over the bald top and put it back on again.

'All right. The boss wasn't always quite so legit,' he said, licking his lips. 'You can't book a man for jobs after he's dead, can you, Inspector?' he added.

'No,' Angel said.

'Well, the boss . . . must be twelve years or more ago . . . used to run a little girlie shop over the bookies next door, until a man called Spitzer, Alexander Spitzer, came on the scene. He was a bad lot from Leeds way. You may have heard of him.'

'No,' Angel lied.

'Don't know what happened to him. Anyway, Spitzer wanted in on it, make it bigger and bring some foreign girls in. The boss was talked into it, I reckon. Anyway, apparently he agreed and Coulson, that's one of Spitzer's boys, brought four girls in from somewhere foreign . . . I don't know where. They jointly bought the old laundry next door, knocked a wall through and began setting it up. Then I heard Myra, his first wife, found out and went ballistic. Also, I think the boss saw his money going out, and not coming back in so soon. Now, I know the boss. He don't like that sort of arrangement, so he wasn't happy. He never really liked Spitzer anyway. He said that he was a bit too flash; also he found out that unbeknown to him, the whole idea was wrapped up in a heavy drugs deal. Spitzer's idea was that the girls could be on their backs at night making money, and in the daytime leaning over factory and school gates and wherever, flogging H. That was going to be great for him at twenty-five quid a throw. And the girls were to get a tenner out of every wrap, Inspector Angel. Think of that! A tenner. Of course, they were up for it. When the boss found out that Spitzer and Coulson was planning this move on the side, he wanted out. He didn't want any truck with them thereafter either. He said he'd rather die than share divs with them.'

'So you think that Spitzer and Coulson might be responsible for Joshua Gumme's murder?'

Makepiece's eyes slid from left to right, then back again. 'No. I never said that, Inspector. I never said nothin' like that.'

Angel pursed his lips.

'OK,' he said knowingly. 'Did Mr Gumme have a gun?'

'I once saw a piece in a shoulder holster. I didn't like that. It was ages ago.'

Angel nodded. He thought as much.

'He was wearing it . . . about the time of this Spitzer business. I haven't seen it for years.'

'Do you know what make it was?'

'No. Don't do guns, Inspector.'

Angel wrinkled his nose.

'Spitzer always had a piece,' Makepiece added. 'He should have worn a bigger jacket.'

Angel nodded, then said, 'What were you doing when this was going on?'

'I was the caretaker here.'

'And chauffeur?'

'No. The boss used to drive hisself then. He drove all the time up to his illness.'

'So who do you think shot Mr Gumme?'

Makepiece shook his head and showed the palm of his open hands.

'I don't know. Lots of folk. The boss made a lot of enemies.'

'What enemies?'

'Well, you see, he didn't intend to. It's just that everything he touched turned to money. Nobody likes to be bested. He used to say that all his competitors were green with envy at the way he built up his business interests. His new house . . . the pool and everything. His new wife. The Bentley. His luck with the cards. He played cards with people and always won and they didn't like it, and they sometimes wouldn't pay up. He hated that. He always chased them down for the last penny.'

'They say he played two hundred games of pontoon on the trot and won every game.'

Makepiece pursed his lips and leaned back. 'That's true. It was in here. At this very table. I was here. And he could have played four hundred games, aye, and more. He was just too tired to go on. His eyes gave out.'

'But he cheated, didn't he?'

'No, sir,' he said indignantly. 'Not that you would call cheating. The judges checked everything out. I wouldn't have called it cheating exactly. He just gave himself an edge. He told me that he never put himself into a situation where he could lose, that's all. He practised that throughout his business life. And that's not cheating, that's logic, ain't it?'

Angel was considering the line of reasoning. There was something there that was not quite right.

'There are some people he would never have played against,' Makepiece added.

'You mean because they would have beaten him?'

'Yes.' He thought a moment. 'The boss used to watch a punter playing cards with someone else. He'd watch them like a hawk for a half hour or so and then he would know, positively. That's all there was to it.'

Angel was certain there was a lot more to it than that.

Makepiece licked his lips and turned away. 'I wanna drink, Inspector. Do you wanna drink?'

'No, thanks.

Makepiece's mouth dropped open. He turned away and looked across at the table of bottles covered with a cloth.

Angel stared at him.

It was hard for Makepiece to look him in the eye. His mouth twitched again.

Angel could not avoid looking at the harelip.

Makepiece looked away. 'Are you sure you don't want a drink?'

Angel wrinkled his nose, looked at his notes and rubbed his chin. 'No, thanks. We've nearly done.'

Makepiece nodded.

'You've been chauffeur for Mr Gumme a long time. You drove his Bentley?'

'Yes. Very proud of his car was de boss.'

'Where were the keys for the car?'

'I had a set which I picked up from the house when I was taking him anywheres.'

'And when you had finished with them?'

'I always dropped them through the letterbox. Ingrid . . . Mrs Gumme no doubt picked them up and put them on the keyboard in their lobby. I would always take them from there when I was taking the boss out or needed to wash the car or anything.'

'So when you returned the car the night Mr Gumme was murdered, you put them through the letterbox as usual?'

'Yes, sure,' he said, wiping his forehead with a handkerchief. 'Sure you don't want no drink?'

Angel shook his head.

'Did you know the car had been found in flames in a field early yesterday morning?'

'No! Who could have done that? If the boss was alive, he'd have had a fit!'

'You know nothing about this?'

'Certainly not, Inspector. Who would want to do a thing like that with such a beautiful machine?'

Angel sighed. Looked at his notes. Wrote something and said, 'I'd better have a look in your printing shop.'

'Oh yeah? Sure,' Makepiece said eagerly. He stood up. 'It ain't that . . . beautiful, Inspector. There's only me goes in there.'

'I'm not from Health and Safety,' he muttered.

Angel followed him out of the office into the racket of the snooker hall. There was the buzz of men chatting, the frequent crack of white balls rattling against colours followed by the thunder of balls rolling round the tables, and, intermittently, bursts of loud, alcohol-fuelled guffaws of laughter. He glanced down the building. Business was picking up. Sixty or more men were now mooching round the tables.

Makepiece walked on four paces to another door in the same wall. With a rattle of keys he unlocked it and switched on the light.

'Come in. There ain't much room. It's a bit untidy.'

Angel looked around. It was about the same size as the office next door but had a large complex machine in the centre that dominated the room. There were machines of all kinds round the walls, presumably for smaller print jobs: folding machines, stapler, a camera, enlarger, a machine with a powerful press for embossing and a powerful-looking guillotine. Everywhere was draped with large menus for Wong's Chinese restaurant.

Angel looked at him and pointed at the menus.

'Just dryin', that's all. Like I told you.'

Angel nodded. It was true.

In a corner were four piles of packets of blank paper, some opened. He also saw an opened box of packs of playing cards with a sample card glued on the outside.

Angel rubbed his chin when he saw them. He reached out, picked up a pack, opened them, took out the cards, fanned about a dozen of them, and peered closely at the back and then at the face side of them. He pursed his lips, screwed up his eyebrows and shook his head. Slowly, he put the cards back in the packet and returned it to the box. He wondered why they were in the printing room.

Makepiece watched him in silence.

Angel turned around. He noticed the spongy uneven sensation of discarded paper underfoot. He looked down to find that he was standing on a half-inch-thick layer of assorted printed waste, guillotine cuts and badly registered pulls, mostly score cards and posters for snooker contests. Angel bent down and delved around underneath. Eventually he stood up, holding several pages of colour magazine quality prints of naked young women in various unusual poses. He pulled a quizzical face and waved them at Makepiece.

He smiled weakly.

'Good, ain't they? I did them. On that,' he added, pointing to the big machine in the centre of the room.

Angel shook his head patiently.

'Notton to do with me,' Makepiece said. 'That was some work the boss brought in.'

Angel let them drop back on the floor and brushed his hands. He then took another look round the room. He didn't think there was anything more to help him with his inquiries. He rubbed his chin. Then looked at his watch. His face changed.

'Well, thank you for that,' he said, making for the door.

Makepiece smiled and blew out a sigh.

'I'll need a written statement in due course. In the meantime, if anything occurs to you that might help me with finding Mr Gumme's murderer, please get in touch.'

'Sure. Sure, Inspector, but I told you all I know,' he pleaded, holding out his hands.

Angel walked quickly through the snooker hall. There were now about twenty tables in use and Bozo Johnson was busy at the bar ringing up money in the till. The place was buzzing with young men mostly with long hair, jeans, T-shirts and trainers, standing around leaning on their cues, talking, sloshing lager or trying to pot a ball. He ignored the sea of unfriendly glances as he weaved his way through them to the door, and out into the street.

SIX

Angel got into his car, drove the few yards up Duke Street to the McDonald's on the corner, then along to The Feathers. He parked up on the car park and pushed his way through the revolving door and made for the reception desk.

A young man in a dark suit came up to him.

Angel leaned over the high desk, flashed his warrant card and quietly said, 'I'm Detective Inspector Angel. I am making enquiries about a man in a wheelchair who visited the hotel at around ten past eight last Tuesday evening.'

'Yes, sir. Would that be Mr Gumme?' he replied promptly. 'I believe he's the only man in a wheelchair who occasionally visits the hotel.'

Angel felt lighter. Gumme was known to the clerk. It was going to be easier than he had thought.

'Did you see him on Tuesday evening, about eight-fifteen?'

'Yes, I believe I do remember him. He arrived here with his chauffeur, but he sent him away, rather rudely, I believe. It seemed a bit odd.'

Angel nodded. That fitted exactly with what Makepiece had said.

'Did Mr Gumme meet with anybody?'

'I think he must have done. We were a bit busy with new guests arriving, so I hadn't my attention on him all the time. He sat over there in his wheelchair facing that alcove with his back to me.'

Angel was quite enthused.

'Who was he with? Who did he meet?'

'I couldn't see, sir. As I recall, they were sat together for some time. But I couldn't actually see who was in the alcove.'

'Was it one person or more?'

'Couldn't really say.'

'And how long were they there?'

'I don't know for certain, sir. We were busy here at the desk from time to time. You will appreciate that it was only when we were not busy that I may have had the time to notice what was happening over there. More than an hour, I would say.'

'But you didn't see Mr Gumme leave with anyone?'

'No, sir. I'm sorry.'

Angel frowned and shook his head.

'The porter may have seen something,' the clerk said, banging his hand on the bell in front of him. 'I'll ask him.'

An elderly man in a plain dark suit and a nebbed hat appeared from among the people coming and going past the desk.

He looked at the clerk.

'Ah, Walter,' the clerk began.

Angel said, 'May I put the question?'

'Of course,' the clerk replied.

'Walter,' Angel said. 'I am a police officer. I am trying to piece together the last hours in the life of Joshua Gumme.'

Walter's eyes brightened. This was a pleasant change from humping cases up and down the place.

'Oh yes. I heard about him being shot and that.'

'He was here on Tuesday evening. He arrived about eight-fifteen and was seated in his wheelchair over there, facing the end alcove. Did you see him?'

Walter thought about it for a few seconds, then said, 'No, sir. Can't say as I did.'

'Didn't order drinks or ask for anything from you?'

'No, sir. I would have remembered.' He pulled an unpleasant face and added, 'I know about Mr Gumme.'

Angel was disappointed.

'Thank you, Walter.'

'Sorry, sir,' the porter said and then vanished into the general throng of people in the hallway.

Angel ran the tip of his tongue across his lower lip.

The clerk said, 'Is there anything else I can do to help?'

'Yes. Let me see the register of guests you had staying here on Tuesday evening.'

'Certainly, sir. We were full, of course. We usually are during the week. We have twenty-eight letting rooms. Most of the rooms are double, but some would be let as single where necessary.'

The clerk turned back two pages of the register, then swivelled the book round to face him.

Angel put his finger on the name at the top and ran his finger slowly down the page. He didn't know what he was looking for. He hoped a name would jump out and jolt his memory, but it didn't.

The clerk watched him thoughtfully.

At length, Angel said, 'I need a copy of this. Have you the facility for copying the whole page including the address column and signature?'

The clerk smiled.

'Of course, sir,' he said and he picked up the book. 'Won't be a minute.' He turned and went into the office at the back of the reception desk.

Angel took out his mobile and tapped in a number.

It was soon answered.

'DS Gawber.'

'Ron, I'm getting a list of the residents of The Feathers the night Gumme was murdered. I want you to go through them with a fine-tooth comb. It might throw up a . . . suspect.'

'Right, sir,' Gawber said.

'And Ron, tell Ahmed I want him to get me a run-down on Benjamin or Bozo Johnson on the PNC. I know he's served time, but I want to know all there is to know. Also his known associates. Got that?'

'Yes, sir. By the way, there was no sign of a pot dog or any of Mrs Buller-Price's stuff in Dolly Reuben's shop.'

Angel wrinkled his nose.

'Well, we can't put any more time into that. I'll be back at the station shortly.'

'Right, sir.'

He closed the phone and shoved it in his pocket as the clerk returned waving two printed pages of A4 and the visitor's book. He handed Angel the pages and replaced the book on the desk.

'Thank you very much for your help,' Angel said as he folded the pages and put them in his pocket.

The clerk nodded.

Angel went straight back to the station and was charging up the green corridor towards his office when he bumped into Crisp sauntering out of CID carrying a file.

Crisp's eyebrows shot up.

'Ah, there you are,' Angel said, looking distinctly displeased. 'How is it I can never find you? You haven't told me how you got on with Edmund Gumme.'

'Haven't really had the chance, sir.'

'You've got a quick chance now,' Angel snapped. 'Did he say he knew about his father's death?'

'Said his father's solicitor, Carl Messenger, had phoned him. He was naturally cut up, but when he heard that he'd left everything to his new wife, he lost interest.'

'Did he have an alibi for the time that—'

'No, sir. Lives on his own. In a flat. He's unmarried. Says he was in bed.'

'What does he do all day, play croquet?'

'He's a teacher. Teaches English at a new school in York.'

'Right,' he said, rubbing his chin. 'Right then, carry on.'

Crisp nodded and turned away quickly and started down the corridor.

Suddenly Angel called out, 'Hey, Crisp!'

He turned back, eyebrows raised.

'Yes, sir?'

'You haven't seen a white pot dog on your travels, have you? A figure of a poodle sixteen inches high?'

Crisp blinked.

'No, sir.'

* * *

'Benjamin Johnson, sir,' Ahmed said, reading from the first of three pages he had printed out from the PNC. 'December 29th 1999. Guilty of manslaughter of Colin Abelson. Hit him with a bar stool in a drunken brawl. Sentenced to twelve years. On appeal, sentence reduced to eight. Released from Durham, 10 January 2004, having served only four years.'

Angel rubbed the lobe of his ear between finger and thumb.

'Anything else known?'

'No, sir. Looks like a clean sheet after that.'

Angel nodded.

'Associates?'

'Horace Harelip Makepiece.'

Angel frowned.

'Shall I read it up, sir?'

'Aye. Make it snappy.'

Ahmed selected the next sheet, cleared his throat and said, 'Horace Harelip Makepiece, born 23 April 1957. There's not much, sir. 1972. Three months' probation for acting as look-out for robbers at an off licence. 1973. Six months' probation for stealing by siphoning petrol from a parked car. 1975. Six months' probation for stealing washing off a clothesline, also fined £100 for taking a vehicle without the owner's consent.'

Angel nodded.

'Anything else?'

'No, sir.'

'Known associates?'

'There aren't any, sir.'

'Right, Ahmed. Now, I'm expecting the PM report on Gumme by email from Dr Mac sometime this afternoon. Keep your eye open for it and let me have a print of it as soon as it appears.'

'Right, sir,' he said. He went out and closed the door.

Angel leaned back in the swivel chair and stared up at the ceiling. He was weighing up the progress he was making on the Gumme murder and was quickly arriving at the conclusion that it was very little. He hadn't a motive, a suspect, a weapon or a clue. There wasn't a scene of crime to mooch around because he didn't know where the murder had been committed. This case was damned unusual. He was still awaiting Dr Mac's and SOCO's report, however. You could never be sure what they might throw up. He had interviewed the victim's wife and the man's chauffeur, but he had not interviewed his only progeny, his son, Edmund. That was clearly his next priority. He was also curious about the parcel left to Edmund by his father. He would like to kill two birds with one stone.

There was a knock at the door. He lowered the chair abruptly.

'Come in.'

It was DC Scrivens.

'Come in, Ed.'

'Is it convenient for me to report on that torched car, sir, Joshua Gumme's Bentley?' the young man said tentatively.

'Yes. Make it quick, though. Who stole it and why?'

'Don't know that, sir. Mrs Gumme was very angry about it. She said that the Bentley had apparently been taken out of the garage during Wednesday night Thursday morning. She didn't know about it being missing until uniform phoned her yesterday morning and she had to go out of the house to the garage to find out for herself. She hadn't heard it being started and driven away. Her Jaguar is kept in the same double garage and that was perfectly all right. Not touched. The garage isn't locked with a key. It's one of those automatic jobs where you press a remote and it opens itself. The remote control and the car key were missing. There were duplicates of both in Mr Gumme's desk. I checked on them; they are still there. She said that the key and the remote used by Mr Makepiece could have been on the carpet by the front door. They would have been dropped there by him, by arrangement, on Tuesday night, after he'd taken Mr Gumme to The Feathers. Maybe with everything happening, she'd not noticed them or forgotten all about them. I surveyed the scene, sir, and I reckon it *might* have been possible to sneak them out through the letterbox with a line and hook.'

Angel frowned.

'A thief would need to know they were there, wouldn't he?'

'Could do it with a mirror on a stick, sir. We know it's been done, sir, don't we?'

'Aye. What else? Any fingerprints, footprints, any forensic?'

'No, sir. I had a SOCO have a look at the front door, the garage and the car. There was nothing.'

'What about the car?'

'Terrible mess. Anything that would burn did burn . . . helped along with a can of petrol.'

'Any prints on *that*?' Angel said quickly.

'No, sir. The kids are getting very streetwise.'

Angel wondered. The door remote and the keys could certainly have been lifted from the hall floor via the letterbox, but he couldn't quite see any of the suspects in the case busying themselves in that way. However, any one of them could have employed someone else to do it. Even so, he couldn't at that point see any motive — only vengeance.

'Right, Ed, that seems to be a thorough job. Ta. Now you can get back to your shoplifting case.'

He nodded and went out.

Angel didn't spend any more time thinking about the torched Bentley, as significant as it might be. It was getting late into a Friday afternoon and there was something he really had to do. He reached into a desk drawer and pulled out the Bromersley phone book. He raced through it and found the number he wanted. He lifted the handset and dialled the number.

A woman with a deep voice answered.

'Carl Messenger, solicitor. Can I help you?' she said in a voice ideal for selling shrouds.

'This is Detective Inspector Angel. Can I speak to Mr Messenger, please?'

'One moment,' she said. 'Please hold on.'

There was silence on the line for thirty seconds or so, then the woman said, 'I am putting you through to Mr Messenger.'

'Good afternoon, Inspector,' the man said. 'How can I help you?'

'Good afternoon, Mr Messenger. I am anxious to make contact with Mr Edmund Gumme. I have his number, but there is repeatedly no reply. I wonder if you know how I might contact him. I understand he is a schoolteacher, but I am not familiar with the name of the school.'

'Nor am I, Inspector. However, I can tell you that he has changed his mind about accepting the small package his father left him. He telephoned me and I have arranged to see him here tomorrow morning. I do not open on Saturdays usually, but I am opening the office at ten o'clock tomorrow especially to accommodate him. Miss Goodchild, my secretary, has kindly agreed to come to the office at that time. You would also be welcome. If you were to attend, you could be one of the two witnesses I will need.'

* * *

'If you would care to sign *there*, Mr Gumme?' Carl Messenger said, handing him a pen. 'Then Miss Goodchild, as witness that the package has been duly received by Mr Gumme . . . *there* . . . thank you . . . then Inspector Angel . . . *there* . . . thank you.'

Angel signed and passed the pen to Messenger. The solicitor placed it on the pen rest and then reached down to the bottom drawer in the pedestal of his desk and pulled out a package, wrapped in brown paper securely sealed with an overabundance of Sellotape. Under the transparent tape, written by hand in black ink on a label, was the one word 'Edmund'. He handed it across the desk to the young man.

'There you are. The formalities are now completed,' Messenger said.

Edmund Gumme took the package with both hands, looked at it and held it reverentially for a moment; he blew across the label, creating a small cloud of dust, read his name written in his father's hand, nodded, then quickly pushed it into his coat pocket.

'I believe our business is concluded,' he said, turning to the solicitor. 'Thank you, Mr Messenger.' He turned to Miss Goodchild. 'Thank you.'

She nodded, picked up her handbag and left the office.

Messenger locked the middle drawer of his desk and withdrew the key.

Gumme looked at Angel and said, 'Perhaps I could have a private word with you, Inspector?'

Angel nodded. He had been hoping for such a meeting. If Gumme hadn't proposed it, he would certainly have suggested it.

They made polite excuses to Messenger and went out of his dismal office, through the waiting room along the corridor to the main door. On the pavement outside, Angel suggested they could sit in his car and talk.

Gumme agreed and when they were both in the car and the doors closed, the young man said, 'I wondered if you had found out who murdered my father.'

'Not yet, Mr Gumme. Not yet. But we will,' Angel said. 'It's early days. Why? Do you have any idea who could have shot him?'

Gumme smiled wryly.

'No, Inspector, but of course, being who he was, he was bound to have lots of enemies.'

'What do you mean?'

'Well, whoever the murderer is, my father probably cheated him in some way . . . either at cards or in his business dealings. My father had the gift of rubbing everybody up the wrong way. I could never get along with him.'

Angel thought it was sad. He had good memories of his own father.

'I'm sorry,' he said.

Gumme sighed and shook his head. 'The trouble was, he wanted me to be a carbon copy of himself: a bullying, tyrannical, self-seeking cheat.'

He paused. Angel said nothing. He went on, 'He called me a "nancy boy" because I liked music, art and literature . . . I didn't want to follow in his footsteps. And when he didn't get his own way, he was intolerable. After Mum died he was impossible to live with. And when Ingrid moved in, my life was unbearable. I simply had to move out. She is a horrible woman, Inspector. You should be warned against her. She only married him for his money. I wouldn't be surprised if she hasn't bumped him off.'

Angel listened carefully. He was hoping for some hard facts from young Gumme that would help him find the murderer.

'It's well known that Dad was like a money-making machine. He had the Midas touch. Everything he turned to made money. Of course, that's all he thought about. She was the same. They were two for a pair. That's at least one thing they had in common. She's not my stepmother. I never accepted her as my stepmother. When she moved in, I moved out. I have not even spoken to her in her role as my father's wife. As far as I am concerned she is a usurper. She should not be in my father's house. She gets the lion's share out of the earnings of his estate.'

'That'll be run presumably by Horace Makepiece.'

'Anything that Horace Makepiece gets, he's earned. My father has been walking all over him for more than twenty years. He's bullied and abused him and made a fool of him in front of everybody. It's time Horace was rewarded.'

Angel nodded. He conceded that the son might be right about that.

'Your father didn't forget you entirely when he made his will?'

Gumme's face showed great sadness. He reached down into his pocket and pulled out the tightly wrapped package.

'I already know that the value of my legacy at the time he made his will was six pounds. So I know that I have not even inherited my grandfather's gold watch!'

Angel said nothing.

Gumme shook the packet angrily then suddenly said, 'Have you a knife or a pair of scissors?'

Angel nodded. He had a small two-bladed penknife in his jacket pocket. He opened the larger blade and passed it across to the young man.

He took it eagerly and began to cut with a sawing action through the several layers of transparent tape around the packet. It took a while and he was getting quite excited as he reached the brown paper wrapper. His face was red, his breathing quicker. His hands were shaking as he made a neat opening in the paper. He handed the knife back to Angel, then he tore open the little parcel. Into his lap fell a pack of playing cards in its cardboard case, a pair of horn-rimmed spectacles with thick lenses, and a small white card. On the card in his father's hand were written the words: *To my son,*

Edmund. Enclosed is the secret to making a fortune. Be persistent, be diligent and you too will become a very rich man. The rest will follow. Your loving father, Joshua Gumme.

Edmund Gumme read the card again aloud, then pushed it in his pocket. His face showed his disappointment. He opened the packet and shook out the playing cards. He took the cards in his hands, fanned them and looked carefully at both sides of them. He selected one card and stared at the pattern, which was a pretty, colourful flower design. He selected another card and put the two side by side. They were identical. He opened up the spectacles and put them on. His eyes took a few seconds to adjust. Then he repeated the previous routine. The back of all the cards looked identical with and without the spectacles. He looked at the face side. There was nothing unusual to see there, with or without the glasses. He shuffled through the cards. Each card was identical at the back and different at the front. At length and with a sigh, he squared up the pack and pushed them back into the cardboard box. He removed the heavy, thick spectacles.

'I cannot see anything unusual about these cards or the spectacles, Inspector Angel,' he said. 'If the cards are specially marked, I cannot detect it; neither with the spectacles nor without them. Whatever mystery these cards may hold is not apparent to me.'

'Your father had some secret which he is clearly trying to pass onto you. There must be something special about the cards or the spectacles or both, Mr Gumme. I understand your father won two hundred successive games of pontoon; lately, I hear, he won every hand of cards he played, without exception. He obviously has left you these cards and these spectacles so that you can do the same.'

'I expect he cheated throughout.'

'Maybe. But it's nevertheless remarkable. Horace Makepiece happened to say that your father told him that his method or system, or whatever it was, did not enable him to beat everybody at cards. There were some people, apparently, that your father could not beat and that he would not play against.'

'He would have said that to save his face for when he lost a game.'

'No. Not at all. He never did lose a game. According to Makepiece, he made a point of observing prospective contenders playing with other people for a few minutes and from that he would know whether he could beat them or not. He would only play against those he could beat.'

Gumme's mouth was turned downwards at the corners. He picked up the wrapping that had fallen on the floor of the car, pushed the pack of cards and the spectacles into it and pressed the jumbled parcel into Angel's hand.

'Very well. You're the detective. See if you can work it out. If I can help you further with your enquiries, Inspector Angel, you have my address. I want my father's murderer caught.'

SEVEN

Angel was back home in a few minutes. He drove the car into the garage and locked it. He dashed into the house and told his wife, Mary, all about Edmund Gumme's legacy and the note his father had left him. He offered her the pack of cards and the spectacles and asked if she could solve the mystery.

She took up the challenge immediately.

'I'll certainly have a go, Michael,' she said with a smile. 'It shouldn't be too difficult.'

Angel nodded.

She examined the backs of some of the cards, sometimes wearing the spectacles and sometimes not. 'The backs of the cards are exactly the same. It is the same pattern on all the cards . . . the same number of petals and leaves and so on . . . in exactly the same positions. There is no difference. They are identical.'

'That's what Edmund Gumme said. And that's what I believe,' Angel said.

Mary thought for a moment. Then she made a suggestion.

'I wonder, if in a certain light, some of the colours of the petals of the flowers in the design on the back of the cards, when seen through the spectacles, might look different, perhaps in some code, displaying the face value of the card.'

Angel pursed his lips. He didn't think that there had been any hand-colouring with special paints on the backs of the cards, but he could be wrong.

'You mean the spectacles acting like a light filter?'

'I don't know technically what I mean, but I wondered if it was possible?'

He was impressed. To that end, they tried various light bulbs and strengths in the house and also outside on the back step in the bright sunshine, but it revealed nothing. The cards looked the same in all the strengths and types of light they could reproduce around the house.

'There's ultra-violet light, isn't there? I've been in shops where they have looked at paper money . . . presumably looking for forgeries.'

Angel rubbed his chin. There were police specialists in printing and forgery: he could consult them.

'I'll send the cards to Leeds,' he said at length. 'To the experts. They have all kinds of sophisticated equipment.'

'And I should take the spectacles to the opticians and ask them if there's anything unusual about the lenses,' Mary said. 'They'll know.'

Angel felt heartened. Certainly Gumme senior expected his son to work out the puzzle. Surely with all the scientific resources of the police force, he should be able to solve the mystery.

* * *

'Mortuary.'

'Good morning, Mac. Michael Angel. Got your report on Joshua Gumme in front of me.'

'Aye, Michael, well?'

'Yes. When you examined his ears . . . I assume you examined his ears?'

'Of course I examined his ears,' Mac said irritably. 'I always make a proper examination of everything at a full postmortem.'

'Well, did you find anything in either of them?'

'No. Nothing. You've got my report.'

'Yes, but . . .'

'What were you expecting me to find? Mrs Buller-Price's pot dog?'

Angel blinked. Even Mac had heard about it. That smart answer left him speechless momentarily. He couldn't think of a clever reply.

'It was a serious question, Mac. Gumme was a notorious card sharp. I simply wondered if he had a . . . a miniature radio receiver of any kind, perhaps disguised as a hearing aid . . . so that an accomplice could . . . maybe have broadcast details of his opponent's hand . . .'

'No.'

'Nothing?'

'Nothing. If there had been, it would have been in my report. There were absolutely no signs of any scientific device fitted temporarily or permanently, externally or subcutaneously, in or anywhere near Gumme's auditory system. Is that comprehensive enough for you, Michael?'

'Yes. Thank you.'

'Now, is there anything else?'

'No.'

'Right then. Goodbye.'

Angel replaced the phone. He sighed. Mac could be difficult sometimes, but he always respected him as a damned good pathologist.

The phone rang immediately. He reached out for it.

'Angel.'

It was Harker.

'Come on down here. Smartly.'

'Right, sir.'

Angel's jaw stiffened. He put down the phone. Harker sounded rattled about something. He didn't think it could be anything in his department. The investigation was admittedly slow, but there hadn't been any calamities he could think of. His team were all engaged in regular, legitimate enquiries and he was broadly satisfied with the way the enquiry was progressing.

He arrived at the superintendent's door and knocked.

'Come in,' Harker roared.

He pushed open the door and found the superintendent sitting at his desk rubbing his hand across his mouth, his eyes flitting from one thing to another and blinking between each stare. Standing next to him was a red-faced DCI Gardiner holding a sheet of paper.

Angel closed the door.

'The DCI wants to ask you something,' Harker growled.

Gardiner said: 'This email came to us from Interpol, Paris. Timed out this morning, Monday 0440 hours.'

He handed it to Angel, who took it and read it.

To all Chief of Polices, Grande Bretagne
From Sureté Agent Dauville, Lyons.

Piper Apache XX2 AB9 originally stolen from Hospitalité Orange de Paris, Orly. Departed Aeropuerto de Madrid, Monday 0418 hours carrying over 110 kilos of heroin thought to be bound for location in Grande Bretagne situate in South Yorkshire. 12 km from Sheffield and 8 km

from Bromersley. Approach with caution. Pilot, Alexander
Spitzer, known to be armed.
    Raymond Dauville, Captain.

Angel gasped when he read it. A hundred and ten kilos of heroin! A big load. A most unwelcome addition to an already over-drugged society.

'If it left Madrid at 0418 this morning, it will be down by now and Alexander Spitzer away by now, sir,' Angel said.

'We know that,' Harker snapped.

Angel said, 'There'll be two possible places that are twelve kilometres from Sheffield and eight kilometres from Bromersley. The northerly one would be somewhere near Tunistone.'

He nodded.

'Right at the top of the rise, near the TV mast, if the Frogs have got it right. There are several farms up there.'

Angel's thoughts flew immediately to Mrs Buller-Price's spread. Her farmhouse was just a stone's throw from the mast.

'Alternatively,' Gardiner said, 'the southerly one is out in the sticks above the Snake Pass.'

'The point is, Michael, do *you* know Alexander Spitzer?' Harker said.

'Yes, sir. Must be ten years ago now. He was a small-time thief when I knew him. I had him put him away for three months for housebreaking. His mother was Czechoslovakian or Croatian or something. She was devastated. Didn't do him any good then. Big drug baron from Leeds way now, isn't he? Served time in Durham, hasn't he?'

Gardiner nodded.

'International figure now. A record as long as your arm. Always packs a gun. Thought to have murdered a man in Andorra. A customs man who got in his way. As sly as a fox.'

Gardiner turned away from Angel and looked across at Harker.

'Right, Michael. That was just to put you in the picture. If you hear anything, let the DCI and me know about it.'

'Right, sir,' Angel said.

'Crack on with . . . that crook in a wheelchair case . . . that Gumme murder, then,' Harker said.

Angel nodded and made for the door. He ran his hand through his hair as he dashed up the corridor back to his own office. They only wanted to see if he knew Spitzer, to see if he would recognize him if he turned up back in South Yorkshire, that's all that was about. Must be ten years since he saw him. He was nothing but an uncouth hooligan then. A young man in a hurry. Now wanted for drug-running and murder and a lot more. He'd seen it all before.

He arrived in his office and immediately picked up the phone. He tapped in a nine for an outside line then tapped in a six-digit number.

There was a click as the phone was answered.

'Hello? Mrs Buller-Price speaking.'

'Ah,' he said. Her voice sounded bright and normal. He was much relieved. 'Inspector Angel here.'

'Ah,' she said warmly. 'How nice of you to call, Inspector. You have some good news for me? You have found my jewellery, my pot dog, my Fifi, and . . . ?'

'Alas, no, dear Mrs Buller-Price, but rest assured we are making dedicated enquiries to find the items, but have had no success up to now.'

'Oh dear.'

'I have really phoned to ask you if you have seen any strangers in the farm or the fields, or indeed anywhere round there, lately?'

'No. I have not, Inspector. I did see your Sergeant Gawber last Wednesday, I think it was. He was very nice, with a fingerprint man. Haven't seen anybody since.'

'I was thinking more recently. This morning? There was a report of a plane getting lost around your way early this morning. You didn't see a small aeroplane . . . ?'

'Must be a rotten navigator to get lost near this thumping great television mast! No. I didn't see any planes. Where was he headed for?'

Angel had to think quickly.

'Huddersfield, I believe.'

'Oh? I didn't know there was a place to land in Huddersfield?'

* * *

'Good morning, Mr Angel. Are Mrs Angel's reading glasses satisfactory? Or is there something wrong with *your* eyes? Is it you that needs an eye test this time?'

'My eyes are fine, as far as I know, Mr Rainford, thank you. As you may remember, I am a policeman . . . a detective. I have a query about a pair of spectacles that have come into my possession in the course of investigating a case. Would you kindly take a look at them?'

Rainford's eyebrows shot up.

'Of course. Of course. How very interesting.'

Angel pulled a large manilla envelope out of his pocket, carefully opened it and slid the spectacles out onto the countertop.

'Ah. Do these belong to a criminal, then, Mr Angel?' he said. He picked them up, opened the arms, held them up in the direction of the shop window and looked through the lenses.

'Something like that,' Angel said.

Rainford turned to Angel and said, 'Now, what exactly do you want to know?'

'Well, is there anything unusual about them?'

'They are not prescription spectacles. Hmm. These are really powerful, unsophisticated lenses for a patient who needs simple magnification, such as for reading or sewing or any kind of close work. The magnification is the same in each lens.'

'Where would one buy these sort of spectacles?'

'From chain stores or multiples or even supermarkets.'

'Is it possible these spectacles have the properties of a filter?'

'These haven't. The lens would have to be tinted or even dark, like sunglasses, to filter out specific colours. As you can see, these are perfectly transparent.'

'Have the frames been interfered with in any way?'

'No. They look as original to me. What exactly do you mean?'

'Has any hearing device like a hearing aid been incorporated in the frame?'

Mr Rainford smiled and made a very careful examination of the two arms and the front of the spectacles.

'You can see that the surface of all the frame is in pristine condition. Just as it would have come out of the mould it was cast in. I have heard of special spectacles made incorporating hearing aids, but these spectacles are very ordinary. These have certainly not been adapted in any way like that.'

'Is the weight of them exactly what you would expect?'

'Indeed, yes. These are a little heavy because the lenses are made of glass. Most spectacles lenses are made from plastic.'

Angel pursed his lips and rubbed his chin.

'Sorry, Mr Angel, I don't seem to have been much assistance.'

'On the contrary, Mr Rainford, you have been most helpful. You have eliminated several possibilities. Thank you very much.'

* * *

'DS Taylor from SOCO brought these in, sir,' Ahmed said. 'There's their report on Joshua Gumme and the contents of his pockets in this EVIDENCE envelope.'

'Right, Ahmed,' Angel said. 'Thank you.'

The door closed.

Angel dived into the folder and scanned through it, sometimes stopping and re-reading parts he found pertinent. As well as particulars of the gunshot wound through the sternum directly into Gumme's heart by a .32, there were details of abrasions in limited areas to his wrists and ankles, commensurate with him being tied to something with rope or tape of some kind. But there were no clues to the assailant or the assailants.

He ran the tip of his tongue across his lower lip and closed the file.

He reached out for the big, manilla EVIDENCE envelope containing the contents of Gumme's pockets, and tipped it out onto the desk. Although most items had been dried out, everything in the small pile was a dirty colour and had the smell and appearance of rubbish from a dustbin. Angel poked about it with a pencil. There was a wallet. It was still damp. He opened it up. There was £400 in notes, some of his own business cards and a card about four inches by two inches. It was a religious tract. It had the picture of an angel on one side and the words 'The Lord shall watch over thee and keep thee safe' on the other. Then in pen at the top were scrawled the words, 'Two million pounds.'

Angel turned the card over, saw the angel, smiled and tucked it back in the wallet. The other items comprised a handkerchief, a small bunch of keys and some coins, but there was nothing there to interest him. He packed the stuff back in the envelope.

He leaned back in the chair and rubbed his chin.

The phone rang.

He leaned forward and picked it up.

'Angel.'

It was Harker.

'Mayfair Security Systems has just reported the triggering of an alarm system of theirs at Creeford Grange. That's where the widow woman of your Joshua Gumme lives, isn't it?'

Angel jumped to his feet.

'Yes, sir.'

'The man said their readouts indicated that someone had gained entry by a rear window and that the intruder was on the premises still. I have sent Hotel Echo One and told them to approach with blues but no siren. Get out there.'

When Angel turned the corner onto Creeford Road, he could hear a two-tone burglar alarm siren making a hell of a racket. He put his foot down on the accelerator and drove straight along the road to Creeford Grange. He raced through the open gates and up the drive. He could see a marked police car, Hotel Echo One, parked right outside the front door.

The siren high up on the front elevation of the house was deafening. He stopped immediately behind the car and jumped out to find a PC racing towards him from behind the house. On seeing it was Angel, he called, 'Oh, it's you, sir. Anybody come that way?'

Angel could hardly hear him above the siren.

'Nobody's come this way,' Angel bawled. 'I'll watch the front.'

'Right, sir,' the PC said and rushed back between the side of the house and the double garage building towards the swimming pool.

Angel watched him go, then suddenly he was startled by a sound and movement close behind. He looked back to see a sleek black Jaguar, its engine purring like a cat gliding to a stop inches from his back. The driver was Ingrid Gumme. She had a face like thunder, her cheeks were scarlet and her eyes flashed like diamonds in the night.

He stepped forward quickly out of her way and continued to watch the house.

Mrs Gumme slammed the car door, glanced up at the blue and white siren high on the front elevation of the house, stormed up to Angel and said, 'What the hell is happening now?'

Angel didn't look at her. He kept looking ahead.

'You seem to have an intruder . . . triggered the alarm.'

Two PCs came out of the front door, pocketing their asps. They had obviously drawn a blank. Angel recognized one of them; it was Scrivens.

They saw Angel with Mrs Gumme and approached them.

'Access has been made into the house, sir,' Scrivens shouted over the siren. 'Kitchen window has been broken. Footmarks scratched the paint on the window bottom. Intruder or intruders wouldn't have been in long, though. Nobody there now. They've been in the bedroom. Dressing table drawers open, stuff pulled out. We'll just check the grounds. If there's nothing there, we'll have a quick tour round the streets nearby. You never know your luck.'

'Right, Scrivens, ta,' Angel said as they ran off.

'Hope they haven't got my diamond rings,' Mrs Gumme said.

Angel pulled out his mobile as he began walking up the stone steps to the front door. He was directly underneath the siren. He stared up at it.

'Can you switch that racket off, please, Mrs Gumme?' he called.

She overtook him and stormed into the house. She went to the small, grey alarm box in the hall, opened the cover and tapped in a four-digit code. The siren stopped: the quiet was a relief.

Angel made an urgent call on his mobile to SOCO.

* * *

The phone rang.

He picked it up.

'Angel.'

'DS Taylor, sir, SOCO. About the break-in at Mrs Gumme's house, sir.'

Angel's face brightened. 'Oh yes, Don. What you got?'

'Nothing much, I'm afraid, sir. I can confirm that the window at the back of the house was the point of entry. The glass was smashed with a long-handled key used for draining the swimming pool. It was standing in the doorway of an outside service room that wasn't locked. There were no prints on it. I think there was only one intruder and I think he must have been quite young.'

'Why do you say that?'

'Size of the shoe, sir. We haven't got an actual footprint. We are working on the size of the graze marks on the wood-work. At the widest, they are only four centimetres across.'

Angel frowned. Sounded very strange. It wasn't likely a young burglar would cut his teeth on a mansion, with a very conspicuous alarm box, in broad daylight.

'I reckon he would only be in the house a minute or two,' Taylor said. 'Was there much taken, sir?'

'Mrs Gumme says everything is accounted for.'

'Sounds fishy, sir?'

'Not fish, Don. Fruit. Maybe a cherry-picker?'

* * *

'Ahmed. I want you to parcel up this pack of playing cards carefully, and get it off to the lab at Wetherby. Mark it for the personal attention of Professor Willington-Atkins. He's expecting it. Put a polite note in it to say it's from me at this address. Send it registered and make sure it goes tonight. All right?'

'Right, sir.'

There was a knock at the door.

'See who that is.'

Ahmed opened the door.

It was DS Gawber carrying a bunch of papers.

'Come in, Ron,' Angel called.

Gawber came in as Ahmed went out; he closed the door.

'Checked through that list of people staying at The Feathers the night Gumme was murdered, sir,' Gawber said.

Angel's face brightened expectantly.

'Oh yes. Sit down. What you got?'

'They check out perfectly, except one. A man who signed the register "Father I. Colhoun, LBOTP, Dunleavy Abbey, County Cork, Southern Ireland." I eventually found the number for the abbey and spoke to the novice master, Father

James. At first he was very suspicious. Seemed to think that I was in some way making mischief. Anyway, he confirmed that they certainly *did* have a Father Ignatius Colhoun; much loved and respected he was too, he said. And that he was in Peru in South America visiting a mission, taking provisions and giving support to a mission out there that was dear to their hearts.'

Angel's mouth dropped open. He rubbed his chin.

'What do the initials stand for?'

'LBOTP? Little Brothers Of The Poor.'

'Ring up the CID Garda in Dublin and ask for their help. Try and get confirmation of what you have been told through them, also see if you can get a photograph of Ignatius wired through. In the meantime, I'll go straight down to The Feathers.'

EIGHT

'Who, sir?' the desk clerk said with a frown.

'A Father Ignatius Colhoun,' Angel said. 'According to your register, he stayed here last Tuesday night, the twentieth.'

The clerk began to turn back the pages of a large book in front of him. As he did so, a look of recollection showed on his face.

'Yes, of course. I remember . . . a man in a dog collar. We don't get many vicars staying here. Only saw him briefly when he registered and again, when he paid his bill the following morning.'

'Ah,' Angel enthused. 'Do you remember anything special about him? What he looked like?'

The clerk looked at Angel with a face as vague as a railway enquiry clerk.

'No. He was . . . tall, I think . . . slim, I think . . . paid in cash.'

'Sterling?'

'Oh yes.'

'Anything else?'

'Nothing really. He was very smartly dressed . . .'

Angel wrinkled his nose.

'Did he speak with any sort of accent? Did he have any facial hair? Moustache, sideburns, beard? Any particular mannerisms?'

'No. No,' he replied thoughtfully. 'Carried a Bible and an umbrella, I remember. He had to hang the umbrella on the edge of the desk to sign the register. He kept hold of the Bible all the time. In his left hand.'

'So he was right-handed?'

'Yes. It would seem so. Have a word with our porter. He might be able to . . .'

He hit the bell sharply twice with the palm of his hand.

Angel nodded. 'Yes. Thank you.'

Old Walter soon appeared from round a corner somewhere and looked up at the clerk then at Angel. He recognized the inspector immediately.

'Back again, sir? Have you got that murderer yet?'

'Not yet, no. But we will. Have no fear. We will. I wonder if you can assist me.'

'I'll try, sir. I'll certainly try.'

'On Tuesday the twentieth, a man in a dog collar booked in here in the name of Father Ignatius Colhoun. I wonder if you can tell me anything about him?'

Walter nodded.

'I can that, sir. Yes. Do you think it was him? Well, anyway, he was a long, sober-faced card. Must have been a bishop at least. Miserable-looking. Dark all round his eyes. He could have got a job in an undertaker's anytime. Very smart black gear he was wearing and a beautiful silver crucifix. And he gave me a very unusual tip. It was a sort of card, with the picture of an angel on one side and a verse of poetry or something like that on the back. I've got it here somewhere.'

He reached into his coat pocket.

Angel realized that the man might be in possession of a clue . . . a vital clue.

'Don't touch it,' he said, his pulse thumping.

'I already have.'

'Well, don't touch it again.'

Astonished, Walter quickly withdrew his hand from his pocket.

'Is it in that pocket?' Angel said.

'Yes.'

'Leave it in there. We might get a print off it. Take your coat off. Let me have it.'

Walter's jaw dropped open. He began threading an arm out of the coat.

Angel's brain raced. He pulled his mobile out of his pocket and tapped in a number. 'Is that SOCO? I want to speak to DS Taylor urgently . . . Very well. I'll hold on.'

Angel held the mobile tightly. As he waited, his mind darted back to earlier that morning. He had found a similar card, as described by the porter, in the dead man's wallet. It sounded identical. If it was, it could help to show that Gumme had been in the company of Father Ignatius (or whoever he was) shortly before the murder. He was delighted. He considered that that was real progress. At last, he had a suspect. And that was good. He rubbed his chin and then sighed. Of course, it was a long way from proving that the priest was the murderer.

* * *

'You don't half take your time, Sergeant. It was Thursday when that postman was assaulted,' Angel said.

'The van was only found yesterday, sir.'

'Burnt out, was it?'

'No, sir,' Crisp said pertly. 'In good nick and with all its load apparently intact.'

Angel's mouth dropped open.

'Did it have any registered mail on board?'

'Yes, sir. The post office checked on that. Thirty-eight items. Half a sackful. All present and correct.'

'But there could have been jewellery, cash . . . all sorts of valuables.'

Crisp nodded.

'Perhaps the thief didn't know.'

Angel shook his head and wrinkled his nose.

'He'd know,' he said meaningfully. 'He must have had a much bigger objective in his sight. He is not your common-or-garden thief. He must have his eye on something much more lucrative or important to him. There's no other explanation. As he isn't stealing the mail, what is he stealing?'

Crisp shrugged.

Angel said, 'Any forensic?'

'No, sir.'

'No prints? No DNA? Nothing?' he enquired heavily.

'Nothing, sir.'

Angel ran his hand through his hair. 'It doesn't make any sense. That's twice it's happened. What's the point of assaulting postmen if you don't want to nick their post, their vans or the money in their pockets? I take it this man wasn't robbed of any personal possessions?'

'No, sir,' Crisp replied. 'Wallet intact. Watch on his wrist.'

'Did you go into the background of the man?'

'There was nothing there, sir. Not known to us. Long-serving employee. Perfect record of service for eighteen years. Besides, as you say, there was nothing stolen.'

'Nothing *found* to be stolen,' Angel said through gritted teeth. 'And how is he? Was he badly hurt?'

'No. Nasty bruise on neck. He had a night in hospital. Everything checked out.'

'Could have been much worse. What happened exactly? What did he see? What did the assailant say?'

'He didn't see or hear anything. He felt a thump at the back of the neck. Next thing he remembered, he was in hospital.'

'Did the house to house turn anything up?'

'No, sir. The attack must have lasted only three seconds. A man walking apparently innocently along the street . . . reaches the postman unloading the letterbox . . . bang, clouts him with something . . . he falls down . . . assailant jumps in his van and drives off.'

Angel growled, then said, 'It's too easy. Too damned easy.'

'Similar to the assault on the postman at Frog's Leap Inn at Midspring on Monday evening. Except the attacker didn't take the van.'

'Is there a connection between the two men? Were they related? Was it the same "walk"?'

'Different "walk", sir. I couldn't find a connection. Been through everything.'

The phone rang.

He reached out for it.

'Angel.'

'It's John Weightman here, sir.'

'Yes, John, what is it?'

'I'm still on the river-bank with the Froggies, sir. DS Stranger has found something. He would like to have a word.'

Angel blinked. It was a surprise so early in the morning.

'Right. Put him on.'

'Good morning, sir,' Stranger said.

'Good morning, Sergeant. What is it?'

'We found a cork float bobbing about, just under the surface of the water, sir, near the bank. It was fastened by a length of cord to a big black plastic bin liner that was half covered in mud on the river bottom. We hoisted it up to the bank. It gave a positive signal on our screen for some metal content. It was waterproof sealed at the neck with sticky tape, so we slit it down the side and found that it contained what looked like a thief's hoard. There is jewellery, silver photograph frames and to weight it down—'

'Don't tell me. There's a white pot dog. Figure of a poodle.'

'That's right, sir,' Stranger squealed excitedly. 'How did you know that?'

* * *

'Come in,' Angel called.

It was Gawber, his face glowing with excitement.

'Report from SOCO, sir,' he said breathlessly as he closed the door.

Angel gawped at him.

'What is it, Ron?'

'They managed to pull a satisfactory print of an index finger from that religious tract you took from the hall porter at The Feathers. It belongs to an Alexander Spitzer, last known address Leeds in 1997.'

Angel's eyebrows shot up.

'Alexander Spitzer! So the great and glorious Alexander Spitzer, the heroin king, is prancing around impersonating a clergyman. Well, well, well.' He sniffed. 'Not a very original idea.'

Gawber agreed.

'That confirms that Spitzer met Gumme the night he died?' Angel muttered.

'Because he had the same religious tract on him, sir.'

He nodded.

'But of course, it's a long way from proving that Spitzer murdered him.'

'It only shows that they must have spent some time together in The Feathers.'

'And we only know about Gumme being in the reception hall.'

'Well, of course, he couldn't have been shot there, sir.'

'Quite. If he was shot in the hotel, the gun would need a silencer and the incident would need to take place behind at least one good, solid door . . . a bedroom or better still, a private bathroom off a bedroom. Even then, it would be hard to believe that someone wouldn't have heard it.'

There was a pause while the two men considered the ramifications.

'What's the "two million pounds" written on the card mean, sir?'

'Don't know yet,' Angel said.

'It's a lot of money if it's a ransom demand.'

Angel shook his head.

'It's a lot of money in any context, Ron.'

Angel eased back the swivel chair and looked up at the ceiling.

'We are looking for a Walther PPK/S .32 automatic. Also Alexander Spitzer. That's a tall order. Interpol have been looking for him for years. Let's have the latest description of him, to remind us all. We have so little to go on.'

Angel suddenly pushed the chair down. He made a decision.

'I want you to have a closer look at The Feathers. Take young Scrivens and go through the room that was occupied by our friend Spitzer. I know the room will have been cleaned and occupied by others since, but nevertheless see what you might dig up. Have a good look in the public rooms, the bar. Ask around. Find out what you can about his mode of transport. How he arrived there and how he left. Talk to the staff. You never know, there might be something you can turn up.'

There was a knock at the door.

Angel looked at Gawber and nodded towards it.

Gawber pulled it open. It was PC Ahaz. He was standing there holding a sheet of A4 paper.

'What is it, Ahmed?'

He put the paper on Angel's desk.

'It's a photograph of Father Ignatius Colhoun of the Little Brothers Of The Poor, sir. It's just come over the wire from the Garda in Dublin.'

Angel looked down at it. It showed a very old man in priest's robes with a biretta.

'Aye, well, that's no surprise. He's nothing like Alexander Spitzer, is he? You can take that down with you, Ron. With a photo of the real thing. You can get that from the NPC. See if you can get a positive ID from the clerk and the hall porter and anybody else.'

'Right, sir,' Gawber said and went out.

Angel turned to Ahmed.

'Now then, there's something I want you to see to. There's a DS Stranger from the Leeds sub aqua team calling in with a black plastic bin liner containing plunder from a burglary, fastened by a rope to a cork float. He should be here in the next few minutes. I want you to take the whole lot straight round to SOCO. DS Taylor is expecting it. Stay with him; I want you to take note carefully how the tape is wrapped round the neck of the bag, and how the rope is fastened to that. Don Taylor is going to see if there are any fresh prints on the bag, the sticky tape or on any of the contents. I have no expectations that there will be. If there are, that's great. If there aren't, I want you take the pot dog round to Enderby's, the glass people. They're expecting it and they'll know what to do. Also, I want you to buy a bin liner exactly the same size and type, and sticky tape the same width and so on as the thief used. Then bring the old bag, the contents, the new bag and the tape back here. If I'm not in, put them in my cupboard here and lock it up. Got all that?'

'Yes, sir,' Ahmed said, rubbing his chin. 'And what are Enderby's going to do with the dog ornament, sir?'

'They're simply going to drill a hole in its backside,' he said bluntly.

Ahmed blinked. His mouth dropped open.

Angel sighed.

The phone rang. He reached out for it.

'Angel.'

It was the civilian telephone receptionist.

'There's a gentleman on the line asking for you. Says his name is Horace Makepiece.'

Angel frowned. He couldn't imagine what he wanted.

'Right,' he said. 'Put him through, please.'

There was a click and silence.

He looked at Ahmed, who was still standing there with a blank expression.

'Well, get on with it, son,' Angel said impatiently. 'Chop chop.'

Ahmed, looking uncomfortable, hurriedly made for the door.

A voice from the phone said, 'Is that Inspector Angel?'

'Yes, Mr Makepiece. What can I do for you?'

'Ah yes. It's maybe sometink I can do for you, Inspector.'

'Oh yes?' Angel said, with a wry smile. In his experience, people with a criminal record, however trivial or serious, never ever made a subsequent approach to the law. The police always had to take the initiative. What was about to happen was a rare exception.

'Yes,' Makepiece began grandly. 'You remember I told you Mr Gumme made a few enemies over the years? Mainly because he was not too subtle at collecting money owed to him?'

'Yes. Yes. Go on.'

'There's a chap the boss played pontoon with some time back. Of course he lost. Lost badly. He had some crack-ball system that if he kept doubling his stake each game he was bound to come out on top. Well, he didn't. He lost his shirt, his building society savings, his car and his house. The man was very nasty and so was his wife. I think he about lost his mind too.'

'Really?' Angel said, trying not to sound excessively interested. 'Well, thank you, Mr Makepiece. I may look into it. Have you got his name and address?'

'His name is James Tasker. I think the wife's a bit lulu as well. Her name's Muriel and they live at 13 Sebastopol Terrace.'

* * *

Angel turned the BMW into the long terrace of houses. He was looking for number thirteen. He passed a young girl bouncing a ball against the wall. When she saw the car, she stopped playing and ran into the house. Two older boys on skateboards whizzed along the pavement giving him a sly glance as they passed. He watched them turn down a ginnel; they probably should have been at school. He came up to a door with the number thirteen in white plastic figures screwed to it and put his foot on the brake. He got out of the car, locked it and went over to knock on the door. It was unnecessary. It was ajar and a young woman's head was peering round it.

'If you're collecting for anything,' she said, 'forget it. We haven't any money.'

'No,' he said quickly, then he reached in his pocket for his warrant card and badge and waved it in front of her eyes.

'Detective Inspector Angel. You must be Mrs Tasker?'

He noticed her eyes bounce as she took in what he had said.

'Oh. Yes,' she said opening the door and standing with one hand on the jamb and the other on the knob.

Angel noticed that she was plainly dressed but round her neck she wore a delicately carved garnet necklace comprising twenty or more small heart-shaped garnets, each in a delicate old gold setting and connected by pretty leaf motif chain links.

'And what can I do for you?' she said assertively.

He looked into her face and waited a moment.

'Can I come in?' he said.

She looked him up and down before replying. 'I suppose so,' she said with a shrug. 'But it's a tip.'

She turned and went into the house; Angel followed. The door opened straight into a tiny living room. It *was* untidy, very untidy, but not dirty. Two small children were playing together in a corner of the room, amidst a pile of soft toys, teddy bears and dolls. Behind them was a door leading to the rest of the house. In the corner was a television set and in the middle was a very well-worn settee and two chairs, covered with toys, newspapers and clothes.

The two toddlers seemed to be enjoying pulling a cord out of the back of a toy to hear an American voice squawk something unintelligible. They both looked up at Angel curiously. He smiled at them. They didn't react, and returned to pulling on the cord.

Angel stood in the middle of the room, looking round.

Mrs Tasker stared at him for a moment.

'Are you wanting to sit down?'

She lifted out some magazines and newspapers from the settee and dumped them in another chair. 'There you are,' she said ungraciously, nodding at the cleared space.

'Thank you.'

'Well, what do you want?'

'Is your husband in?'

She hesitated. 'No. What do you want him for?'

'Routine enquiries, Mrs Tasker. Where abouts is he?'

'I don't know.'

'Is he at work?'

'He doesn't work,' she snapped.

The door behind the children suddenly opened and a man in a vest, trousers and slippers came in. He needed a shave. He glared at Mrs Tasker and then at Angel.

'He works when he can get a proper job,' the man growled, 'but I think the word is out that James Tasker is unemployable.'

He strode carefully over the heads of the two children and took up a position in front of the fireplace. They ignored him. He looked down at Angel.

'You a policeman?'

'DI Angel. I'm looking into the murder of Joshua Gumme.'

Tasker shrugged.

'So what are you doing here?' he said roughly.

'I am trying to contact all the people who had reason to dislike Mr Gumme.'

Mrs Tasker said, 'Dislike? *Dislike*? We didn't dislike him, Mr Angel, we hated him.'

Tasker looked at his wife.

'Yes,' he said. 'It's about the only thing we have in common, now. That and the children.'

His wife nodded.

'And *you're* not getting *them*,' she snapped.

Tasker ignored her.

'You will have heard why we have cause to hate him, I take it? That's why you're here.'

'You played cards with him and lost,' Angel said.

'He didn't just lose a game of cards,' Mrs Tasker said. 'He lost our house, our home, our car, our savings and our future. He gambled everything on the turn of a card. He needs his head looking into. What we saved and earned over twelve years, he managed to give away to that monster in a few hours.'

Tasker glared at her.

'All right! All right!'

'The solicitor says the debt didn't die with him. Even now, we still owe his estate — that tart — over eighty thousand!'

'Muriel! Change the record. It's true. It was stupid. But it's done now.'

'Do you want to tell me what happened?' Angel said quietly.

'I can do,' he said, running his hand through his hair, 'but I can't do it with *her* interrupting at every verse end—'

'Oh, get on with it!' she shouted. 'You like talking. That's all you do.'

The two children looked up at her. The youngest was about to cry. Angel recognized the signs. The child looked like he felt.

Mrs Tasker dashed over to her. 'Oh, now then,' she said to the tot. 'Mummy didn't mean to shout. It's your father!'

She picked up the young child, looked back at Angel and unexpectedly said, 'I suppose you'd like a cup of tea? Milk and sugar?'

Angel looked at her brightly.

'Ta. No sugar,' he said.

She nodded.

'Come along, Adrian.'

She went out through the door, carrying the younger and holding the hand of the other who toddled unsteadily with her.

'Now then, sir,' Angel said, looking up at Tasker.

The young man's face tightened.

'Yes, well, there was all this stuff in the papers about how wonderful this man, Gumme, was. How he could outplay everybody. So I just simply offered to play him. I knew — or I thought I knew — that his luck couldn't possibly hold. He couldn't possibly win *every* game, one after the other. I had a strategy. If it wasn't going well, I would wait to win just one big hand and then leave the table. I realized that I might lose a hundred pounds or so, but I expected *that* to be the very worst outcome. I really thought there was a chance of me winning a fortune. After all, pontoon is mostly a game of chance. But it didn't happen like that, because I never had a good hand. He always had the aces, the court cards and the tens. I kept going because I thought my luck would turn. I employed the doubling of the stake plan. You know, if you lose, you double your stake each hand. It is a sound theory, but you still have to win a game. I simply didn't win a single game. Of course, he was cheating, but I couldn't see how. I looked round for mirrors. There weren't any. I kept my cards closed and close to my chest, in case he had an accomplice, and I covered the backs, but it still didn't make any difference. The betting went on and on. I fully expected to win the next hand. He couldn't possibly win every hand. But he did. It was awful. After I had lost everything, I insisted on examining the cards, but I couldn't see anything unusual about them. I even counted them; there were fifty-two of course. I don't know what I had expected. Those thick specs he wears, when he took them off, I looked through them. Very strong lenses they were, but that's all.'

'Where did this take place?'

'In a sort of office at the far end of the snooker hall.'

Angel nodded. He knew the place.

'It must be worth a fortune to know how he did it and kept on doing it,' Tasker said. 'And it all happened so quickly. I hardly dare come home to Muriel. I knew we would have to leave our detached house on Creeford Road, and hand the car in and . . .'

Angel thought a moment.

'Why did you want to take on such a gamble in the first place?'

'That's another story. I was gainfully employed, Inspector, as assistant manager at the Bromersley branch of the Yorkshire and North Lincolnshire Building Society on Duke Street. I was doing rather well. I thought I would be there for life. I'd been there ever since leaving school. Passed all my exams. When it was taken over by the Northern Bank last January, they hadn't a job for me here. I could have had a job at a lower grade in Todmorden, but Muriel didn't want to move. It would have been that bit further away from her mother, so I found myself out of work. I have tried everywhere to get a job at the same level but there's nothing turned up as yet in Bromersley.'

Angel nodded.

'Do you own a gun?'

Tasker's jaw dropped open.

'A gun? No.'

'You've never owned a gun?'

'No. Never.'

The door opened and Mrs Tasker came in with a tray with two cups of tea on it. She turned the tray at an angle and offered it out to the two men.

Angel took the cup nearest to him.

'Thank you,' he said.

Mr Tasker picked up the other cup without comment.

'Has he finished his stupid, *pathetic* tale then?' she said, looking at Angel.

Tasker growled and turned away.

'I've another important question,' said Angel. 'Where were you both on the night of Tuesday, 20 March between eight o'clock and, say, nine o'clock in the morning?'

'We were here,' they both said in unison.

'Can anybody verify that?'

'We can verify each other,' Tasker said.

Angel wrinkled his nose. That wasn't quite a twenty-four-carat alibi. Husband and wife giving each other an alibi.

His wife looked at him, pulled a face like Medusa and said, 'I was here, Mr Angel. *All night*. Where else could I possibly be?'

NINE

'Yes, Ahmed? What is it?'

'An itemized list, from the phone company, sir. All the calls made from Joshua Gumme's house phone over the past two weeks, arrived second post, sir,' Ahmed said.

'About time,' Angel sniffed.

'I've traced each one, sir. There doesn't seem to be anything helpful to the investigation. Most of the calls were to retail businesses in the town or to the snooker hall or to Makepiece's flat,' Ahmed said, putting the two A4 sheets of paper on the desk. 'It confirms that Mr Gumme last rang the snooker hall at 20.05 hours the night he was murdered.'

Angel nodded and looked down at Ahmed's handiwork.

'That fits in with his call to get Makepiece to come round and take him to The Feathers.'

The phone rang.

He reached out for it.

'Angel.'

It was the superintendent.

'Come down here. Straight away!' Harker bawled and banged down the phone.

Angel sighed. Sounded as if he was breathing out fire again. He ran his tongue across his lower lip. He jumped up and pushed the list back into Ahmed's hands.

'I have to go. I'll have a look at it later.'

'Right, sir.'

Angel dashed out of the office and up the corridor. He wondered what had happened to upset the dragon. Or was he just going to crack the whip again? What was he so worked up about? It's true he wasn't moving very effectively with this Gumme case, but considering the dearth of clues and lack of DNA he didn't feel he was doing too badly.

He knocked on the door and pushed it open.

'Aye. Come in,' bellowed the man with the turnip head, red face and staring eyes. He was seated at his desk and holding a pink expense chitty. He thrust it across the desk at Angel.

'This yours?' he said.

Angel took it, glanced at it, looked back at Harker and said, 'Yes, sir.'

The superintendent looked sneeringly at him.

'This isn't the fancy goods department at Debenham's, you know,' he said, his hands shaking and his bushy eyebrows twitching. 'Read it out, Inspector. Read it out.'

Angel sighed.

'I know what it says.'

'Read it out. *Aloud.*'

Angel's lips pressed tight against his teeth.

'It says, "to drilling quarter-inch diameter cavity in white pot dog, £10.00".' He looked across the desk into his red face. 'It's from Enderby's, the glaziers, sir. They're the only people who would do a job like that, and they didn't damage the dog at all.'

He put the paper back down on the desk.

The superintendent winced.

'They didn't damage the dog at all?' he bellowed. 'I can't approve an expense like that! If you want to make a bloody table lamp out of a piece of Mrs Buller-Price's pottery then you'll have to pay for it out of your own pocket.'

Angel's eyebrows shot up.

'But it's not for that!' he said.

'Whatever it is, I can't pass it,' Harker snorted. He reached forward, picked up the chitty, screwed it up and threw it in the waste-paper basket at the side of his desk.

'But I've already paid it,' Angel explained.

'That's hard luck. I am surprised at you trying to get that past me.'

'I wasn't trying to get anything past you.'

'That's all I have to say on the matter,' Harker said. 'I've no time for this nonsense.'

He shook his head and waved a hand to change the subject.

'This is a police station not a pot shop,' he muttered, then added, 'How far have you got with these attacks on postmen?'

Angel sighed, shook his head and said, 'They're dead ends, sir. I haven't got anywhere.'

Harker stared at him. An occasional flickering reflection of the ceiling light on his spectacle lenses reminded Angel of old clips of film of Heinrich Himmler.

'Nothing seemed to have been taken,' Angel added, 'and there doesn't seem to be a link between the two men.'

'You must have missed something. It doesn't make sense.'

Angel agreed but he wasn't going to admit it.

There was a pause.

'What about the gun in this Gumme murder?'

'I've had an underwater team searching the river for a week but there's no luck so far.'

'If they can't find it in a week, they'll never find it.'

Angel knew he was probably right.

'Call them off,' Harker insisted. 'Save us a few hundred quid. I have to pay for the frogs out of our own budget, you know. They don't turn out for us for nowt.'

Angel nodded.

'I have to go down there in the morning, sir. I'll make a decision about it then.'

'Call them off now!' he bawled. 'Cut your losses.'

* * *

'Come in,' Angel called.

The office door opened and Ahmed came in carrying the pot dog under his arm. He looked very clinical wearing white rubber gloves.

'Good morning, sir.'

'Good morning.'

'I've brought this down from Traffic, sir.'

'Aye. Put it down there,' he said with a nod.

Ahmed carefully placed it on Angel's desk.

'It's all ready, sir,' he said as he turned back and closed the door. 'DS Mallin said he'd fitted it himself. He's checked it out and it's transmitting now.'

'Good. I hope it's not been chipped at all.'

'It looks perfect, sir. The sergeant has covered over the hole in its bottom with a bit of plaster of Paris. You can hardly see it.'

Angel had a look at the back end of the dog and nodded approvingly.

'Right. I want you to put all the swag, including the dog, into the new bag; squeeze out the air, then seal it up with that sticky tape exactly as it was . . . fasten that rope with the float on to it, just the way Harry Hull did it. I want it to look as if it's not been touched since the night he dropped it into the River Don. And make sure it's watertight. Can you do that?'

'Yes, sir,' Ahmed said with a grin. 'It's a wicked plan.'

'He's a wicked man. Crack on with it. I want Crisp to take the whole shebang back down to the river this morning and get the froggies to place it back in the water exactly where they found the original.'

* * *

Angel stopped the BMW outside 101 Earl Street, a big, old house in need of a coat of paint. He went up to the door and pressed the bell. He didn't hear it ring so wondered if it worked. He pressed it again. Then he heard the loud clatter of footsteps down uncarpeted stairs; the door was opened by a middle-aged woman. She glared at him indignantly.

'What do you want?' she snapped. 'You're *not* the postman.'

He frowned. He knew he wasn't.

'I'm looking for Mr Harry Hull.'

'That must be the new tenant,' she said. 'Flat two. Up the stairs. First door on your left. Follow me,' she said.

'Thank you.'

She turned round and ran back up the stairs. Angel followed. She pointed at a door and then rushed off along the landing and round a corner out of sight.

Angel reached the door. It had a strange symbol in black on it. He reckoned that it must be a figure two painted by a man with St Vitus' Dance.

He knocked on it.

It was opened only two inches.

Angel could only see a nose and an eye, but it was enough for him to recognize that it was the man he was looking for.

'What you want?' a voice said.

Angel put all his weight against it and pushed. The door and the man behind it moved backwards until it was wide enough to gain access.

'Here, here. What you doin'?' Harry Hull shouted indignantly.

'Don't you recognize an old friend when you see one?' Angel said as he closed the door behind him.

Hull stared at him uncertainly and then relaxed.

'Yeah,' he said sneeringly. 'It's old St Peter hisself . . . Detective Inspector Michael Angel . . . come to make my miserable life even more miserable.'

'Now that's where you're wrong, Harry.'

'Huh. I doubt it. You needn't have been so aggressive. I would have let you in . . . even though you haven't got a warrant. Cos I ain't got nuthin' to hide.'

Angel glanced round the little room. It was probably true. There wasn't any room to hide anything.

'Cosy little place you've got here, Harry.'

'Smells a bit since you got here,' he said. 'But it's all right. Anyway, what's a big cheese like you tripping round small fry like me? You could have sent one of your boys.'

'It's called goodwill, Harry. Goodwill.'

'Huh. I'll believe that when I see it.'

'Yes. It's a new policy. We reckon that if we can help our . . . ex customers to get settled back into the community, they're less likely to reoffend.'

'That what the probationary service wallahs are paid to do. They're a thick load of nerks, but they look better and do it better than bigfoots like you. You must be up to something, Angel. What you after?'

'Have you got a job yet?'

'No. Are you offering?'

'Have you tried?'

'Of course I've tried. But as I am obliged to tell a prospective employer that I've just come out of Armley, that . . . sort of . . . puts them off.'

'It would,' he nodded. 'It would.'

'The probationer wallah is finding me something in a factory soon, she told me. The pay's peanuts but it's a start. Huh!'

'As it happens, Harry, I do have a little job you could do for me. It would be a sort of job on commission. Because of your . . . background, you are in a unique position to assist me.'

'Oh? What's it pay?'

'A hundred pounds.'

Hull sniffed.

'A hundred nicker? That's not much these days.'

'You haven't heard what it is. And that's only a start. I simply want some information. I want you to ask around your . . . friends and acquaintances.'

'Yeah. What?'

'Well, a week last Tuesday, Harry, thieves broke into a farmhouse near here and stole some expensive jewellery, some antique silver and a very valuable pot dog, about sixteen inches high, the figure of a French poodle sculpted in white china by the famous seventeenth-century Greek artist, Aristo Hypotenuse. Now the haul seems to have disappeared off the face of the earth. The police and the insurance company have searched everywhere for it, but without success. They are particularly concerned about the sculpture.'

121

The pupils of Hull's eyes moved slightly to the left and then back to the central position.

Angel knew he had his man.

'Yeah. So what?' Hull said.

'It's worth a great deal of money, Harry. It's irreplaceable. I don't suppose you have seen it on your travels, have you?'

'A white pot dog? Of course not. How much did you say it was worth?'

'I didn't. And it isn't just a white pot dog, Harry. It hasn't got an actual price tag on it, but if it was auctioned in one of the international houses, it could fetch fifty thousand pounds, or even more.'

Hull rubbed his scratchy chin.

'Fifty thousand smackers.'

Angel visualized the cogs going round in the evil little villain's mind.

'Here,' Hull suddenly said. 'Fifty thousand smackers! And you're only offering me a hundred quid?'

'You talk as if you already know where it is,' Angel replied carefully.

'Eh? Oh no. No. I was just thinking, it isn't much.'

'All I'm asking you to do is point to the party who has it, wherever it is. That's all. You never know, in a pub or somewhere, you might hear people talking. They might not think much to it. They might not appreciate the skill and artistic eye required to translate the beautiful lines of this dog, a French poodle in this case, into china without losing any of its naturalness.'

'Well, would whoever has possession of it now be arrested?'

'They certainly would,' Angel said robustly. 'And be very firmly dealt with. They should hand the sculpture into the police immediately and take whatever punishment is coming to them. It would be a charge of housebreaking and stealing; that would be an absolute minimum of three years. I tell you, Harry, that's what I would do.'

Hull frowned and sighed.

'However,' Angel continued, 'what the thief will probably do, is pass it on quickly to a fence for the best price he can get. That would be the surest way of him staying out of prison.'

Hull nodded.

'What you thinking, Harry?' Angel said, smiling.

* * *

'Come in,' Angel called.

Ahmed burst into the office excitedly waving a sheet of A4.

'Just come through, sir!' he said, his eyes bright as he placed a telex on the desk in front of him. 'Thought you'd want to see it straight away, sir. It's about Alexander Spitzer.'

Angel picked it up.

It read:

To all 43 UK police forces, Metropolitan, Interpol and MI5, cc Home Office.
From DI Thorogood, investigating officer, Mantelborough Police, West Yorkshire.

Information about the whereabouts is sought in connection with Alexander Spitzer, 38, aka Fr Ignatius Colhoun and Luke 'Fingers' Coulson, 36, who, after a short exchange of handgun fire outside a transport café on the outskirts of Mantelborough, in which an officer was wounded in the shoulder. The wound is not thought to be life threatening.

Spitzer is also wanted in Spain for murder, and both men are wanted for possession of eighty kilos of Class A drugs, for the purposes of sale and distribution.

DI Thorogood of Mantelborough CID urgently seeks any information re whereabouts of these two men. Telephone 22394 297223.

Angel re-read it, nodded, then rubbed his chin. He was pleased that Spitzer had been seen. It might prove helpful to his investigation of Gumme's murderer. He felt a warm tremor of excitement in his chest as he thought about it.

'Hmm. Ta,' he said. 'I shall deal with that in a minute, Ahmed.'

The young man beamed.

'I've got a little job for you,' Angel continued. 'I've been thinking about this for a while now. I want you to go to the general post office on Victoria Street and speak to the manager; tell him I want the scheduled routes of the vans of the two men who were assaulted. I want to know the precise streets and roads they were to traverse, and the times they should have reached and cleared each letterbox. Then I want you to mark it up on a street map, and set it up here on that wall behind me. OK?'

'Yes, sir,' Ahmed said.

'Right,' Angel said. 'Now off you go, then. Chop chop.'

Ahmed smiled and dashed off.

Angel watched the door close then he reached out for the phone and determinedly tapped in the number. He felt that he might be on the verge of a breakthrough. It couldn't come too soon.

The phone was soon answered and he was quickly passed from the Mantelborough police receptionist direct to DI Thorogood.

'This is DI Angel at Bromersley CID, I have your message down the wire. I can tell you that Alexander Spitzer aka Fr Ignatius Colhoun was staying at The Feathers Hotel here in Bromersley on Tuesday night, 20 March.'

'That's great,' Thorogood said. 'But are you sure it was him?'

Angel wrinkled his nose.

'He was in priest's clothes handing out Bible tracts. We got a fingerprint from such a thing; it was Spitzer all right. He was believed to have met a local man, who the following morning was found dead, shot in the heart. I am interested in finding the man's murderer. Obviously, Spitzer might have been responsible, but, as yet, I have nothing firm with which to charge him.'

'That's interesting. Did you say The Feathers Hotel in Bromersley?'

'Yes. I have a sergeant working there at the moment. I understand that Spitzer wounded one of your men? Sorry about that. Can you say what sort of gun he was carrying?'

'It was a Smith and Wesson .38.'

'Thank you.'

'Was Luke Coulson with him?'

'No. Never heard of him. I don't think he's from round here. Spitzer was born in Leeds, I believe.'

'I don't think he was born,' Thorogood said. 'I think he was hatched.'

Angel had the same feeling.

'Right. Thanks for your help.'

'Thank you for yours, and good luck.'

'Goodbye,' Angel said and replaced the phone.

He rubbed his chin. The water was getting muddier. Nothing was getting any clearer.

The phone rang. He reached out for it.

'Angel.'

'It's me, sir. Ron Gawber.'

Angel thought he sounded breathless, as if he'd been running.

'Yes, Ron?'

'I found a gun, sir.'

Angel raised his head.

'Where?'

'In the cistern of one of the lavatories in the ground floor of the Gents.'

Angel understood his breathlessness. He felt his own pulse thumping. Maybe this was the breakthrough he had been hoping for.

'Looks like it's been dumped in a hurry. It's not wrapped in anything. Got it out with a coat hanger. It's drying out on some newspaper.'

'What's the make?'

'It's a Walther PPK/S .32 automatic.'

TEN

Angel stopped the BMW opposite the illuminated flashing 'Snooker' sign. He locked the car and walked under the sign down the snicket to the door. It was wide open, as it had been before, and it was busy and noisy. He could hear loud echoing voices and the click-click-click of balls as they crashed into each other on the green baize. As he walked into the hall, he noticed that most of the tables were let: the grey covers were off and the powerful lights above were generating heat. The young men in T-shirts with snooker cues, some drinking, some chatting, who bothered to notice him, turned distinctly sour: he was an older man trespassing in a young man's world. The pressed suit and collar and tie made him stick out like an orchestra leader at a jumble sale.

He looked up at the bar. Horace Makepiece was leaning over the counter reading the *Racing Post*, while Bozo Johnson was removing tops off bottles of Fosters for two racy young men with ponytails.

He stepped up to the bar.

The till bell rang as Johnson pressed the keys.

He stood right in front of Makepiece, who suddenly looked up from the list of runners and saw him. His jaw dropped, then he smiled.

'Hello again, Inspector,' Makepiece said evenly. 'What can I do for you? Did you wanna see me?' He began to fold up the newspaper. His face suddenly straightened. 'You haven't got the bloke what done it, have you?'

Angel shook his head.

'Not yet. I'd like to have a private word with your Mr Johnson,' he replied, nodding towards the big man.

The pupils of Johnson's eyes slid momentarily to observe Angel, then quickly returned to the young man he was serving.

Makepiece hesitated.

'Wid Bozo? Sure. Sure,' he said and he turned to the big man.

Johnson passed some coins to his customer, who had lively-looking tattoos of snakes spiralling down from under his short shirt sleeves to the back of his hands. The young man then picked up a glass of something from off the bar and wandered away sipping it.

'Hey Bozo,' Makepiece said, 'the inspector wants to have a private word wid you. Take him in the back office? Yeah?'

'Right, boss,' Johnson said and rubbed his mouth very hard. He picked up an opened can of Grolsch, took a swig, emptied it and threw it into a bin under the counter.

He passed behind Makepiece to get to the counter gate, pushed it open and came down into the body of the hall. He nodded at Angel and made his way through the customers between the tables to the far end of the hall, glancing back to check that Angel was still following.

They were soon in the back office. Johnson switched on the light and closed the door. It looked exactly the same as it had looked the previous Friday, when he had interviewed Makepiece.

Johnson looked at Angel.

'This all right, Inspector?'

'Yes. Fine.'

Angel sat in the same place he had chosen before, facing the door. Johnson sat opposite him.

He was a big man.

'Your name is really Benjamin Johnson, isn't it?'

'Yeah. It's only really the boss, Mr Gumme, and now Harelip that calls me Bozo.'

Angel nodded.

'Why was that?'

'Dunno. I didn't mind.'

'Did you like Mr Gumme?'

He pulled a face. 'Yes.'

'You didn't, did you?'

He hesitated. 'I didn't like him taking the mick out of me. I mean Bozo is the name of a clown. Who wants to be named after a clown?'

Angel nodded.

'But of course, he sort of . . . bought the privilege,' Johnson continued. 'He gave me a job as assistant manager. It was a leg up. I mean, I'd never been a manager before.'

'Especially at a time when nobody else would employ you?'

Johnson raised his eyes. His face went red. His lips tightened against his teeth.

'That bastard Harelip's been shooting his mouth off again, hasn't he?'

Angel blew out six inches of air.

'Well, we know that you've served time, Mr Johnson. It's a matter of record.'

'Yeah. Yeah. And I can never get away from that, can I?'

Angel blinked. He was stuck for a suitable reply. He wanted to change tack.

'I need to talk to you about Mr Gumme. I want to know what you were doing the night he was shot.'

'Yeah. Well, I was here until ten-forty or so. Unusually, Harelip had been called out to run him somewheres at eight-ish. He got back at a quarter past. We close at ten, so I cleared the tables and checked the lavatories. There were a few drunks outside kicking up. I went out and chased them off. Then I locked the doors, cashed up, prepared the money for the bank, cleared and covered all the tables and everything. Then Harelip and me closed up and dropped the money in the night safe together, which is only next door, and then we parted company. I went home. I only live round the corner. Harelip lives at the back of the hall.'

'You married?'

'No. I live on my own . . . at the moment. I had a relationship going but I packed it in a couple of weeks back.'

'You were on your own until the following morning?'

'Yeah.'

'And Mr Makepiece, does he live on his own?'

Johnson smirked. 'Yeah. Huh. I reckon he'd need a face change for a woman to take up with him.'

Angel considered the comment. It was true he was no oil painting, but he'd seen worse with some most attractive women.

'Do you own a car?'

'Yeah. I got an old Merc. Don't get out with it much though. Working all hours, you know. But got to have decent wheels to pull a bird, don't you?'

'Have you any idea who might have wanted to kill Mr Gumme?'

'Well, frankly, Inspector, just about everyone. He was decent enough to me, but he got his money's worth. I mean, I work about fifty-six hours a week. It isn't heavy work, but it's tying. I'm always here at ten in the morning. I have four hours off in the afternoon . . . when Harelip's always there. Then I'm here until we finish, normally about a quarter past ten. Harelip's fed up with the long hours. When he's not in the hall, he's driving the boss around. And the boss treats him like dirt. He don't seem to notice.'

'But that's not a motive for murder?'

'No. No, it isn't. I didn't mean that. It could have been anybody at all who owes him money. His collection technique is very . . . rough. Very rough indeed.'

'What do you mean?'

'Harelip'll tell you. He threatens and bawls and puts the fear of God into anybody and everybody.'

'Yes. I see. And who owes him?'

'Everybody he's played pontoon with.'

A mobile phone began to ring. It was Angel's. He dived into his pocket.

'Excuse me,' he said to Johnson, then he stood up and turned away from the table. The LCD told him it was DS Mallin from Traffic Division.

'Angel speaking. What is it, Norman?'

'The tracer shows that your pot dog is on the move.'

Angel's eyes lit up.

'Ah,' he said enthusiastically.

'And at a very slow speed, sir. So I take it the thief would be walking.'

'Which direction is he taking?'

'We picked up the first sign of movement at Town End Bridge about five minutes ago. That would be when it was pulled out of the river. The flasher now indicates that he is halfway up Sheffield Road . . .'

Angel frowned. That was not in the direction of Harry Hull's flat. 'Right, Norman. I'll ring you back in a few minutes.'

He cancelled the call and immediately dialled another number.

A voice answered. It was Gawber.

'Yes, sir.'

'Ron. I've just heard from Norman Mallin that Mrs Buller-Price's dog is being taken for a walk and that it is half-way up Sheffield Road. I want you to check it out now. You know what Harry Hull looks like, don't you?'

'Oh yes, sir.'

'I'm on my way. I'll come in the other direction. Don't want to lose him. You might beat me to it. I'm in Earl Street. I am leaving now.'

He cancelled the call, closed the phone, pocketed it and turned to Johnson.

'You will excuse me. Something's come up. I have to go to see a man about a dog, Mr Johnson. Thanks very much. I'll get back to you if there's anything else.'

Two minutes later he was in his car, chasing along Cemetery Road. He made the corner and started up the far end of Sheffield Road. There was no sign of Harry Hull. Then he saw Gawber's car coming towards him. He lowered his window and signalled him to stop. Then he pulled out his mobile and dialled out Mallin's number.

Gawber stopped at the opposite side of the road, unfastened his seat belt, opened the car door and rushed across the road.

'Have you seen him, sir?' Gawber called.

'No,' he growled back. 'I'm phoning Norman Mallin.'

There was a click in the earpiece and a voice answered.

'Yes, sir?'

'Norman, are you still getting a signal?'

'Yes, sir.'

'Well, where is he now?' he yelled.

'At the bottom of Cemetery Road,' Mallin said.

'The bottom of Cemetery Road?'

Angel had a flash of inspiration. He looked at Gawber.

'He'll be at Dolly Reuben's. Maybe he doesn't know Frank Reuben's in Pentonville.'

'That's it!' Gawber yelled. 'He'll be trying to fence the stuff there.'

'Thanks, Norman,' Angel said, his pulse racing. He closed the phone. He turned back to Gawber. 'I'll meet you there. Give me time to turn round. Then you take the front door. I'll take the back.'

Gawber nodded and dashed back to his car.

Three minutes later, the two cars pulled up a little way from the front of the grubby, insignificant little shop which had the hardly distinguishable words *Frank Reuben Second-hand Furniture* in peeling green paint on a cream background over the dirty shop window that had been splashed with dirty rain-water by passing vehicles the past six months or so.

Angel got out of the BMW and rushed along the pavement past a hairdresser's shop and a greengrocer's and up a ginnel.

Gawber waited on the pavement, counted up to sixty and then shot quickly into Reuben's shop. The old-fashioned bell jumped like a monkey on a stick when it was clouted by a metal projection screwed to the top of the door. The cluttered little shop was piled high with old, dusty chairs, tables and rolled-up carpets. No human was in sight. Gawber heard a scuffling noise in the back room. He went straight through to see big Dolly Reuben standing hands on hips with her back to a fire, the back door opening and Harry Hull with a big suitcase walking straight into Angel's arms.

'Oh, hello, Harry, are you just leaving?' Angel said. 'Don't you know it's bad manners to leave just as someone arrives — it looks as if you don't enjoy their company. And what have you got there? My, that's a big case. Are you going on your holidays? I should let Sergeant Gawber take a look inside it. He'll make certain you haven't forgotten anything. It would be a shame to get all the way to Strangeways or Pentonville and then discover that you've forgotten something. Like a pot dog, for instance.'

Hull's jaw dropped to his navel and then came back up again.

* * *

'It certainly looks as if he was possibly shot with his own gun,' Dr Mac said. 'The calibre matches and it had been fired recently.'

'Any fingerprints?'

'No.'

Angel rubbed his chin.

'Right, Mac. Thanks very much.'

He replaced the phone and turned to Gawber, who was sitting opposite him.

'Gumme shot with his own gun,' Angel muttered, shaking his head.

'Hard to believe,' Gawber said.

'Yes. Say Gumme drew his gun and made threatening noises . . . for some reason . . . the party overpowered him . . . I don't suppose it would have taken much . . . took the gun from him and shot him at close quarters straight through the heart.'

'It could have happened like that, sir, I suppose,' Gawber said.

'Yes. But where?'

'Anywhere.'

'No, Ron. Not anywhere. Not in The Feathers. Not in that reception room off the entrance hall.'

'Too many people.'

'And it would have made too much noise.'

'Maybe in a bedroom . . . Spitzer's private bathroom would be the best bet. Did you have a good look round there?'

'Yes, sir,' Gawber said.

'Let's take another look.'

* * *

'Good afternoon, Inspector,' the clerk at the reception desk said. 'You're getting to be a regular visitor.'

'I wish it was a pleasure, but it's work, I'm afraid. You know my sergeant, of course?'

The two men exchanged nods.

'I would like to take another look at the room occupied by the man . . . Father Ignatius Colhoun,' Angel said. 'He stayed the one night, a week last Tuesday.'

Ah yes,' the clerk said, turning back the pages of the big book. 'Room 102.' He turned round to the keyboard, unhooked the key and passed it over the counter. 'The first floor. I'm sorry. I'm afraid you'll have to walk. The lift's out of order again. It's only one flight. Turn right at the top.'

Angel smiled. 'Thank you.'

That was no problem. The two policemen made the stairs easily and were soon outside room 102. Angel put the key in the lock and opened the door.

The room seemed very comfortable, clean and airy and had all the usual offices almost to luxury standard. The bed was made and there was no luggage or clothes visible.

Angel began to systematically search the room. He crouched down to start at the skirting board, then he examined the door frames, the window frame, the furniture, the carpet and the walls for any damage that may have been made in the course of a fight or even by a stray bullet.

Meanwhile, Gawber, who had searched the hotel with Scrivens the previous day, stood patiently in the middle of the room with his hands in his pockets. He licked his lips anxiously as Angel checked what had already been done; he only hoped he hadn't overlooked anything.

Angel moved the bed and the two bedside tables, but found nothing. Any ledge or rim he couldn't actually see, he ran over with his fingers. He stood up and went into the bathroom. He pulled the light cord. It was tiled from ceiling to floor. He scanned it meticulously with a torch from his pocket, but there was no damage at all. He went back to the bedroom. He pulled back the bedspread and looked at the pillows. There were two plump ones. He picked them up and thumped them several times.

He turned to Gawber: 'Nip out and find the chambermaid, Ron.'

Gawber went out and reappeared with a woman in a white coat. When she saw Angel feeling down the stripped mattress and the blankets draped over a chair her face went pink and her eyes almost popped out of her head.

'What's going on?' she stormed, rushing towards him. 'I've finished this room. It was all ready for occupancy. What do you think you are doing?'

Gawber smiled.

Angel said, 'There's nothing to worry about, dear lady. The room is immaculately serviced and spotlessly clean and tidy. You are to be congratulated. We are humble policemen making enquiries into a criminal who stayed here recently that's all. And I need to know if you were responsible for cleaning this room on Wednesday last.'

'Of course I was,' she said, pouting. 'There *is* only me, since Muriel Tasker left, and she wasn't much good anyway.'

Angel blinked. Gawber's mouth dropped open. They exchanged glances.

The chambermaid said, 'Now what have I said?'

Angel licked his lips. 'It's nothing of importance. We happen to know the lady, that's all.'

'You'll know that she's round the twist then, won't you? Anything that wasn't done right on this floor and the floor above was nothing to do with me.'

'Muriel Tasker used to work here, then?'

'Only temporary. I think she only wanted the job to get something on that poor husband of hers.'

'Why? Did he work here?'

'Nar. But he had been known to come here for a quiet drink . . . to get away from her, I shouldn't wonder. She used to ask questions about him, and everybody else. She took pills for her head. I'm not surprised. Ready for a straitjacket, she was.'

Angel ran his hand through his hair. This was going to lead him down a line of inquiry he thought had been closed, as if this case wasn't complicated enough.

'Now what did you want me for? I've four more rooms to do. Visitors will be arriving any time. I must get on.'

'Yes,' Angel said, collecting his thoughts. 'I wanted to ask if you found anything untoward in this room? In particular, any damage to the bedding, the pillows or anything else.'

'No, sir. They wouldn't dare in The Feathers. It's too well respected.'

'You're sure? Have you never had to replace a . . . pillow here, for instance, or have you ever had a pillow stolen?'

'No. Never. Now move out of the way and let me put that bed back to rights. The occupant for this room might arrive at any moment.'

ELEVEN

Angel and Gawber made their way down the stairs to the reception desk. The clerk came up to them.

'Have you completed all your inquiries, gentlemen?'

'Not quite,' said Angel. 'You had an employee, a Muriel Tasker?'

The clerk wrinkled his nose then raised his eyebrows. 'We did, yes. She was a chambermaid. She was only here eight days or so. She didn't last long. I think she thought she was too good for the job. Apparently she had two small children and wasn't too happy with her babysitter. She left very abruptly . . . without working her notice. Mr Turnbull, the manager, was not very pleased about it.'

'Did you know her husband?'

'Yes,' he said brightly, his eyebrows shooting up again. 'Nice chap. Well, he used to be. But he changed. Used to be very pleasant and friendly. A good mixer. Was in the habit of spending a lot at the bar, I believe; now more likely to buy a half and sit in a corner on his own looking at it for an hour or so.'

'Was he in a week last Tuesday night, the twentieth?'

The clerk frowned.

'I've no idea. Can't remember. Lot of water passed under the bridge since then, Inspector.'

'That was the same night Joshua Gumme was here: the man in the wheelchair,' Gawber prompted.

'Yes. I remember seeing *him*,' the clerk said. '*He* doesn't come in that often, but Mr Tasker, I really don't know.'

'And Mrs Tasker?' Angel asked.

'Yes. She was here.'

Angel and Gawber exchanged glances. Angel felt his pulse rate increase. Gawber gave a small sigh.

'She worked a split shift. All the upstairs staff do. They service the bedrooms, bathrooms and corridors on two floors from eleven till three, then room service or waitressing in the public rooms depending how busy we were from six until ten.'

Angel said, 'So Mrs Tasker could have been in this reception area the night Joshua Gumme was murdered?'

'Yes,' the clerk said.

* * *

A few minutes later Angel and Gawber came out of The Feathers Hotel.

Angel felt a bit taller and a bit lighter afoot. He was distinctly encouraged by what he had learned about Muriel Tasker; it was heartening that two of the three requirements of a crime — motive and opportunity — seemed, at last, to have come together. He needed to establish the third, the means, and then he knew he had a possible murderer of Joshua Gumme in his sights.

He stopped under the hotel portico, sniffed, looked at his watch and turned to Gawber.

'It's four-thirty, Ron. I'm going on to see the Taskers. You go back to the station. See if there's anything known on the PNC re James and Muriel Tasker, and give me a ring on my mobile.'

'Right, sir.'

'Tomorrow, I want you to see if you can find anything, anything at all, about their previous lives. Talk to their old neighbours up Creeford Road. Check on their days at school and since. See his old boss at the Yorkshire and North Lincolnshire Building Society. See if she worked before they were married. You know what to do. At the moment, Ron, I feel as if I am dealing with shadows. I don't really know anything about these people. I like to know the sort of people I am dealing with. If you have a known villain on your hands, you know exactly what to expect. The way I feel at the moment is that the murderer is very close, very close indeed, but could slip through our fingers like quicksilver.'

Gawber knew exactly what he meant.

'I'll phone you as soon as I've had a look at the PNC, sir.'

Angel nodded.

Gawber dashed off to his car, unlocked the door, started the engine and drove away.

* * *

Angel pulled up outside 13 Sebastopol Terrace.

He knocked on the door; it was promptly opened by Mrs Tasker.

'Oh, it's you. Back so soon, Inspector?' she said coolly, standing on the step with her arms folded.

141

He didn't reply. He just looked at her. He knew that he might be looking into the face of a very dangerous woman.

'You'd better come in,' she said, grudgingly. She pulled the door open more widely.

'Thank you.'

The room was just as it had been the day previously. The two children were still playing in the corner on a pile of toys and still pulling the cord out of the back of the squawking doll.

She indicated the chair as before.

Angel sat down. He ran his tongue round his mouth and then said, 'I won't beat about the bush, Mrs Tasker.'

She sat down in the opposite chair and looked across at him.

'You didn't tell me you used to work at The Feathers.'

Her eyebrows shot up; her jaw stiffened.

'You didn't ask me,' she snapped. 'There's no crime in it.'

'In particular, you didn't tell me that you were there the night Joshua Gumme was murdered,' he said quietly. 'You said you were here, with your husband.'

'That bitch of a first and second floor chambermaid must have been shooting her mouth off.'

Angel said nothing.

'So you have immediately jumped to the conclusion that I had something to do with his death, I suppose. Well, I didn't.'

'Why lie about it, then?'

She cast her eyes momentarily to the ceiling.

'I don't want every Tom, Dick and Harry to know that my husband had been sacked from a highly responsible managerial job, got himself tanked up and had gambled away our house and home and just about everything else, and that consequently, I was reduced to working as a domestic in a hotel to try to put some food on the table!'

She was red in the face and breathing heavily.

Angel waited a few moments for her to settle down.

'Did you see Joshua Gumme that night?'

'No.'

He waited, then shook his head.

'Can I have the truth . . . from now on?'

'Yes. Of course.'

'Did you see Joshua Gumme that night?'

'Yes. He was talking to a Roman Catholic priest from 102, at a table in one of the alcoves in the reception hall. Huh! Gumme talking to a *priest* of all people! I saw him from behind a rubber plant by the lift. I hated him. Oh, how I hated him.'

'Did you approach him?'

Her mouth dropped open. 'Of course not! Do you think I would have let him see me in a domestic servant's stupid overall?'

'You didn't approach him?'

'*No!* I've already said so, haven't I? I didn't go anywhere near him. You can ask that priest.'

Angel only wished he could. He hoped that one day soon he could question Spitzer at close quarters.

'What were they doing? Were they drinking?'

'I don't think so. Didn't see any glasses or cups or anything. Just talking. Couldn't see Gumme's face. He had his back to me. Looked like the priest was angry about something. He was doing most of the talking and getting angrier and angrier . . . waving his arms about.'

'But you had no idea what they were saying?'

'No. Too far away.'

'How long were you watching?'

'About five minutes, I suppose. I was getting very upset . . . just watching him. I was getting all worked up. I admit I would have liked to have gone over to him and gouged his eyes out, I was so angry. I had a pain like as if I had a half-brick where my heart is . . . and I was . . . I was crying . . . and I *never* cry . . . I had to leave. I couldn't stay there; besides, a few people were giving me funny looks. I went back up the stairs to the linen room. I had to hide my face from the young couple in 106 coming down.'

'And what time was this?'

'I don't know,' she blurted out wildly. 'I don't know. I've no idea. I was looking at the man who had ruined my life. I was half out of my mind. I hadn't got a stopwatch on him.'

'Approximately?'

'Nine o'clock, nine-thirty.'

'And what time did you leave the hotel?'

'Straight away. I couldn't stand being there a moment longer.'

'What time did you get home?'

'Ten o'clock about.'

'Do you know what happened to Gumme after that? I mean, what time did he leave? And how did he leave? Someone must have taken him.'

'I don't know, Inspector. I have no idea. That was the last time I ever saw him. And good riddance.'

'And where was your husband while you were at The Feathers?'

'Here,' she replied. She nodded towards the corner at her two children, quietly playing. 'Somebody's got to look after them.'

'He was here when you returned?'

'Of course. Then he went out.'

Angel nodded. He thought for a moment.

'Where's your husband now then, Mrs Tasker?'

Her mouth tightened again.

'In a pub somewhere, I expect.'

A phone rang out. It was Angel's mobile. He stood up, dived into his pocket and turned away.

'Excuse me,' he said.

It was Gawber.

'Yes, Ron,' he said. 'What have you got?'

'Neither of them is known to us, sir.'

'Right.'

'But I've been thinking. Isn't she the woman who was an actress? Muriel Fitzwilliam, her name was. Lead in that heavy television series, *Love Is My Revenge*. Victorian upper-class family who murdered each other. My wife raved about it at the time. Muriel Fitzwilliam, if it is her, gave up acting to get married. Her father and mother were in the same line, I believe . . . never made it big, though.'

Angel turned and looked at Mrs Tasker.

She was leaning over one of the children, straightening his clothes. She sensed he was watching her and glanced back at him with dark, disturbing eyes.

He imagined her with appropriate make-up and hairdo, close-fitting black clothes, bustle and button-up boots.

'Yes,' he said uncomfortably. 'You're right.'

* * *

'Good morning, sir.'

'Come in, Crisp,' Angel said. 'At last, I've found you. You're harder to find than John Prescott's secret store of pies.'

'I've been helping Ahmed to draw up the maps of those "walks" on that post office job.'

Angel blinked.

'Are they finished?'

'Almost.'

Angel puffed out a mouthful of air. He shook his head and said, 'Well, here's a proper job for you. I want you to find out who was Gumme's doctor. You can ask Mrs Gumme. Find out what was the matter with his legs. Just exactly how disabled he was. I want to know how much walking he could do. How dependent he was on that wheelchair. I want to know whether he could, say, walk up a flight of stairs or not.'

Crisp screwed up his forehead.

'Right, sir,' Crisp said. 'Do you think he's faking?'

He turned to the door then came back.

'How is that going to help us, sir?'

Angel shook his head patiently.

'It closes down some of the options open to us, doesn't it? Disposes of some of the possibilities. If he really *could* walk, even a short way, he could be in places that presently we assume he could *not* be. All right?'

Crisp frowned.

Angel sniffed.

'Just find out, Crisp, old son,' he said, waving his hand impatiently. 'Just find out for *me*. I know this is a stupid, puzzling nonsense of a case. At present, just about everybody involved had reason enough to murder him, and just about everybody could have done it, too. So we need all the facts we can muster; then we can eliminate those that don't progress the case, and what we are left with, hopefully, will be enough to pinpoint the murderer. Then *I'll* be happy, the *super* will be happy, and we can all draw our wages, go home and celebrate with a glass of water and a wine gum. All right? Now buzz off!'

'Right, sir.'

Crisp went out as Ahmed came in.

'What is it, Ahmed?' Angel growled.

'The post, sir. And there's a packet from the lab at Wetherby,' he added brightly, placing the bundle of envelopes down on the desk.

Angel's face changed. He stood up and reached out for it. There were several envelopes of different sizes, which he tossed to one side. He seized the small packet, which had a registered label on it from National Police Laboratories and was marked 'URGENT' in red. He tore open the padded envelope and tipped out the contents: the pack of cards and a letter. He unfolded the letter.

Dear Inspector Angel,

I return herewith the playing cards you submitted and have examined them most carefully.

I have subjected both sides of the cards to examination using filters of a full spectrum of colours, also ultra-violet and infra-red, and have found no reactions whatsoever.

I can confirm that the florally decorated backs of all the fifty-two cards are, in every particular, identical. There is no possible question of the cards being 'marked'.

I trust that this assists you with your investigation.

Yours truly,

J. Willington-Atkins

Professor Forensic Medicine MA, BSc

Angel threw the letter down on the desk, ran his hand through his hair and bounced down in the swivel chair.

Ahmed said, 'Bad news, sir?'

With a wave of the hand, he indicated to Ahmed that he could read it.

He did so and then put the letter back on the desk. He didn't know what to say. He decided to wait and say nothing. It was a sensible decision.

Eventually, Angel said, 'It does *not* assist us with our investigation, Ahmed, does it? I have had Joshua Gumme's glasses at the opticians. There is nothing unusual about them. They are merely strong lenses that anybody might buy from a chainstore. They are not prescription lenses and they do not incorporate any filter. They would be excellent, I suppose, for sewing, knitting, reading and playing card games . . . so that you don't miss any detail of the play . . . so that you can see the cards and the stake money clearly. But I fail to see any other part they play in aiding the wearer to win at the game.'

He sniffed.

Ahmed nodded.

He reached down to the pack of cards, opened the box, took out the cards and began to feed them one by one from one hand to the other, looking at the back of each card in turn.

'Now,' Angel continued, 'Professor J. Willington-Atkins has examined these cards and has declared that the backs of these fifty-two cards are identical in every particular in all lights and all filters. That totally rules out any possibility of an optical trick or marked cards. The face side *has* to be different, of course.'

He turned the pack over.

Ahmed frowned.

'Why can you not accept, sir, therefore, that the cards are genuine?'

'Because Gumme always won. He won consistently with these particular cards. There are more than a hundred packs of cards exactly like these in the printing room at the rear of the snooker hall. I don't understand why they are kept in a print shop, if no additional printing or marking is required to be done to them. It beats me. Those packs are all brand new, as supplied by the maker. Furthermore, Gumme willed this particular pack to his son. And there was a note that accompanied the cards and the specs. Just a minute.'

Angel squared up the cards and put them back in the box. Then he reached into his inside pocket and pulled out several used envelopes with his small writing scrawled all over them. He searched down several until he found what he wanted. 'I wrote it down at the time, as I remembered it. It was in Edward Gumme's father's own hand. This is what the note said: "*To my son, Edmund. Enclosed is the secret to making a fortune. Be persistent, be diligent and you too will become a very rich man. The rest will follow. Your loving father, Joshua Gumme.*"'

Ahmed looked at Angel intently. He was clearly moved. It was like being spoken to from the grave.

Angel put the envelope back in his pocket. He reached forward for the pack of cards.

'There is something different about these cards,' he said, holding them between thumb and forefinger and waving them at Ahmed. 'These cards hold the secret to Gumme's amazing ability to win *every* time he played pontoon, and I mean to find out what it is,' he said, then he pushed the pack into his jacket pocket.

* * *

Angel drove slowly through the open gate up to the farmhouse door. He pulled on the handbrake, switched off the ignition and got out of the BMW. The cold whine of the Pennine wind was overtaken by the distant barking of Mrs Buller-Price's five dogs. Then suddenly the front door of the house opened and the throng of excited canines burst out to greet him. He looked up and framed in the doorway nearly filling it, was the smiling proprietor herself. He acknowledged her with a wave of a hand, as he opened the car boot and took out a black polythene bag.

Mrs Buller-Price's hands went up and her face broke out into a big smile.

'You've found my rings and my photographs and things, haven't you? Oh, I knew you would. Do come in. I have a friend visiting me. She used to help me in the house years ago. Did you manage to recover everything, dear Inspector Angel? My photographs?'

He smiled.

'Everything on your list, Mrs Buller-Price.'

'Oh, that's wonderful. Come in. Come in.' She looked at the dogs barking around Angel's knees. 'Now, you chaps must be quiet. Settle down.'

They did.

She closed the front door.

'Come on through, Inspector. Would you please put the swag on the table in the kitchen? That's wonderful. Thank you. It will be all right there. I'll go through it later. By the size of it, you must also have Fifi, my pot dog. That's wonderful!'

'I'm afraid Fifi has suffered a little damage at her rear end.'

'Never mind. It doesn't matter. I only looked at her face. I am so pleased to have her back. And all my other things. The photographs! You have no idea. Now please, Inspector, come through into the sitting room.'

He stood at the door and saw a small elderly lady whom he thought he recognized. She was sitting near the fire holding a cup and saucer and balancing a plate on her lap. She looked up at him and smiled. He returned the smile and nodded.

'That's it,' Mrs Buller-Price said. 'I'll get another cup. You like the chair Alistair Sim always chose. Please sit there, if you would like to . . . next to my friend. Oh, I must introduce you.'

Angel smiled.

'Alice,' she said. 'This is Inspector Angel, my very good friend.' Then she turned to him and added, 'Inspector, this is Mrs Gladstone.'

They shook hands.

'Pleased to meet you,' she said sweetly. 'Are you a policeman?'

'Yes, indeed. Pleased to meet you, Mrs Gladstone.'

Angel looked at her closely. Her face was familiar. He rubbed his chin. He couldn't recall where he had seen her before.

Mrs Buller-Price said, 'Mrs Gladstone used to come and "do" for me, many years ago, when my dear Ernest was alive, didn't you, Alice? You couldn't get a more honest and conscientious help. We must have known each other forty-five years. We go on church trips together sometimes, don't we, Alice?'

Mrs Gladstone nodded.

'Yes. Last month, we went to Whitby for the day.'

'That must have been nice,' Angel said, not knowing what else to say.

'I'll just get another cup,' Mrs Buller-Price said, making for the kitchen. 'Tell the inspector your good news,' she called over her shoulder. 'What you have just told me. I am sure he'd be most interested.'

Angel looked at Mrs Gladstone attentively.

The old lady smiled back at him.

'Yes, well, you see, my daughter has bought a villa in Spain, and we are moving out there in November this year. So we won't have to face another English winter. Isn't that nice?'

'Indeed it is,' Angel said. He wrinkled his forehead. He'd seen her somewhere.

Mrs Buller-Price returned with a cup and saucer and began to pour out the tea.

'You'll be coming back for the summers, won't you, Alice? So we won't lose touch.'

'Oh, dear me, yes. I hope so. My daughter says she has to come back to work. Although the villa is paid off, she will still need to work to keep both houses going.'

Angel took the tea. The memory segment of his brain was racing faster than the meter on a London taxi.

'Help yourself to cake, Inspector,' Mrs Buller-Price said.

'Thank you,' he said, selecting the thickest slice of Battenburg on the plate.

'And what does your daughter do, Mrs Gladstone?' Angel asked with a skilled, airy casualness he had perfected over years, as he bit off a measured mouthful of cake.

'Oh, Gloria is a school dinner lady.'

Gloria! It came straight to him. Of course! The old biddy was the mother of Gloria Swithenbank, whose house he had searched for Class A drugs only a week ago.

He beamed and thoughtfully reached out for another piece of cake.

'A dinner lady? How very interesting.'

TWELVE

Half an hour later, Angel arrived back at the station. He made his way slowly up the corridor, his trouser belt feeling more than satisfyingly tight, the result of the intake of four scones and two additional thick slices of Mrs Buller-Price's Battenburg.

Ahmed recognized the footsteps and dashed to the open door of the CID office to catch him as he passed.

'The super's looking for you, sir,' he said, biting his lip. 'Sounds as if something has upset him.'

Angel growled.

'There's always something upsetting him. Right, Ahmed. Ta.'

He turned round, went back down the corridor straight to Harker's office, knocked on the door and went in. The monster was at his desk apparently sorting through three large piles of paper. He glared up at him over his specs.

Angel felt a cold east front coming direct from the Barents Sea.

'You wanted to see me, sir?' Angel said gruffly. He thought if there was trouble coming, it might be a good idea not to seem to be on the defensive.

Harker blinked, snatched off his spectacles and leapt up from his chair. 'I most certainly do,' he snapped.

Angel's eyebrows shot up. He was surprised at the extent of his antagonism. He couldn't begin to imagine the reason for it.

'Sit down,' Harker barked, pointing to the chair facing the desk. He then reached forward to a small pile of papers under a glass paperweight depicting an ancient scene of a scaffold in Strangeways Prison. Angel could see that from beneath it, the superintendent's blue, bony fingers were pulling out a sheet of A4 with the words, 'National Police Laboratories' printed at the top. He pulled the document out with a flourish and thrust it at him.

'What's that all about?' he snarled, his hand quivering.

Angel quickly glanced at the paper. It was an internal invoice charging Bromersley Police Force £40 for full-colour optical tests on a pack of playing cards.

'It's self-explanatory, sir. I authorized it. It was necessary to try to determine exactly how the victim, Gumme, managed always to win every time he played the game of pontoon. I have a suspect, a Mrs Muriel Tasker—'

'I've read all about her. Have those tests been helpful in progressing your case against this . . . Muriel Tasker?'

'No. Not against her. The tests have made certain eliminations as to how Gumme managed to cheat everybody—'

'Do we *know* Gumme cheated everybody?'

'Not exactly, sir. I cannot yet prove it. But it seems very likely. Pontoon is mainly a game of chance and Gumme is reputed to have played games where he has won every single game in a sequence of two hundred games.'

Harker seemed taken aback.

'Really?' he said thoughtfully.

Angel noticed the dragon's fire was abating.

'If and when I can discover how he managed to cheat, I believe it will enable me to discover his murderer.'

'Hmm. But it was her husband, James Tasker, who was the gambler and lost their house and everything, wasn't it?'

'Yes, sir.'

'Go on.'

'Well, she seems much more vital and vindictive than her husband. But nothing is clear cut yet. They could be in it together. Incidentally, if I am able to prove that Gumme cheated the Taskers out of their property, then an appropriate claim will be able to be made against his estate.'

Harker nodded slowly.

'Of course. Coming back to this cheating business . . . Did you say Gumme won every game that he played?'

'Yes, sir. But there is one proviso. I understand from his driver . . . manager . . . friend . . . I don't know what to call him . . . Horace Makepiece, that Gumme wouldn't play everybody. He always watched prospective mugs play other people first. But if he *did* play against them, then he would certainly win.'

'Amazing,' Harker said, leaning back in the chair. 'Whatever could he observe by simply watching them play?'

Angel shook his head.

'I don't know.'

'Something psychological, do you think?' asked Harker.

'It's something more practical than that, I think. Psychologists make mistakes: Gumme never did.'

Harker rubbed his scratchy little chin briefly, then suddenly his face brightened.

'Hmm,' he said grandly. 'We seem to have a classic case then . . . of a man who couldn't lose.'

Angel thought for a moment, smiled and said, 'But he did lose, sir. He lost the biggest game of all.'

'Oh,' Harker said. 'What was that?'

'He lost the game of life, sir.'

Harker smiled.

Angel's jaw dropped. He had seen the superintendent smile. Harker never smiled. It was thought to be a bad omen. It was said in the police canteen that every time Harker smiled, a donkey died!

* * *

Ten minutes later, Angel came out of Superintendent Harker's office and made his way thoughtfully up the corridor, content that he had dealt with old Grumble Bum satisfactorily and congratulating himself that he had not been provoked into saying anything he would have regretted. He had long since given up the prospect of ever reaching a sensible, cooperative relationship with the tyrant, so sustaining the existing sort of armed truce was about as much as he could hope for. Over the years, he had calculated a sort of allocation of info to pass on to the superintendent in reports or verbally, on a need-to-know basis. In that way, provided that he had judged it accurately, he would always — so far as his case work was concerned — have the upper hand.

The old plan was working perfectly.

He arrived at his office to find the door wide open and Ahmed there holding a clipboard and checking off coloured markers on two large maps on the wall behind the desk.

'Aye — aye, Ahmed. What's all this?' he said, peering up at the maps.

Ahmed turned round.

'Sir?' he queried.

'I see,' Angel said, moving nearer to the wall. 'You've prepared a separate street map for each "walk"?'

'Yes, sir.'

'And what's the scale?'

'Two inches to a mile, sir.'

He nodded with satisfaction. That was big enough for him to read the street names.

'And these small yellow stars I have stuck on represent the letterboxes,' Ahmed explained enthusiastically. 'I've written on each star the time it was to be cleared or emptied each weekday, Monday to Friday. And I've indicated in yellow, with arrows, the route and direction the postman had to take. You will see that the times progress by a few minutes each box. Now the first postman was attacked on Monday 19th at 7 p.m. out in the countryside. That's this map on the left. And the second man was attacked on Thursday, 22nd at 2.50 p.m. That "walk" . . . detailed in the same way, on the map on the right. Now the actual letterboxes where the men were assaulted, I have marked, respectively, with much bigger yellow stickers.'

Angel stared at the two maps and rubbed his chin. He liked what he saw.

'Yes, yes,' he mumbled.

'I don't know if you have any queries about it, sir?'

'No, Ahmed,' he muttered, absorbed in the detail. 'Ta.'

Angel ran his finger up and down the route marked out on the map and tapped thoughtfully with one finger, the yellow star representing the letterbox where the postman had been attacked on Thursday 22nd. He traced it round the map, reading the stickers, and then suddenly muttered, 'Edmondson's Avenue 12.45?'

There was a short pause, then something remarkable happened to him. Realization dawned. He tapped his temple with an open hand, then turned round to Ahmed, his eyes staring.

'Edmondson's Avenue 12.45!' he cried. 'What an ingenious idea!'

Ahmed looked anxiously at him. It wasn't the DI Angel he knew and loved.

Angel's face was illuminated like a WIN on a one-armed bandit. His eyes glazed over as he imagined a line of six-foot blondes in sequin dresses, twirling pompoms, high-kicking their way through his office accompanied by a uniformed forty-five-piece brass band.

'Ahmed. Get me DS Gawber straight away.'

'Are you all right, sir?'

The girls and the band disappeared as quickly as they had come, but Angel's heart was still banging away.

'Yes. Yes. Get me DS Gawber,' he snapped, wiping his forehead with his handkerchief.

* * *

Three hours later, Angel was standing in his office in front of the maps. He was not a happy bunny. He was rubbing his chin and running the tip of his tongue along his bottom lip when there was a light tap on the door.

Angel quickly turned round.

It was Gawber. He came in quietly and closed the door.

Angel raised his head and stared at him.

'It's all set, sir,' Gawber said.

Angel sighed.

'Are they using a vehicle that looks like a telephone engineer's van?'

'Don't know, sir,' Gawber said. 'I didn't want to hang about with them. The fewer, the better.'

'Yes. That's right. I hope they are not using that damned butcher's van again.'

'You worry too much, sir.'

Angel shook his head and looked him square in the face.

'If this op goes belly up, Ron, my career in the force will be over. For you, there's no problem. You can just say you were obeying my orders. That would be right. And that's OK. But for me, it would be finished. And I am not the sort of man that could ever get accustomed to walking an Alsatian round a builder's site in the middle of the night, I can tell you.'

'They'll have that CCTV camera up there in no time, sir. They've done it a thousand times. Maybe more. They're the experts. Might even be up there working now.'

'You told him I wanted it to catch the face of the person *and* the package the instant it is being shoved into the letterbox?'

'Yes.'

'And that I want it in focus? I don't want a blurred picture that some smart arsed barrister can argue is that of the ghost of Lily Savage and not Gloria Swithenbank.'

'He knows, sir.'

'And I want surveillance for, say, thirty-six hours. That means applying a night lens. Do they know that?'

'I told them.'

'Where are they putting the van with the monitor and recording gear?'

'They're parking it on a woman's drive who doesn't have a car, three doors away.'

'You gave him my mobile number?'

'DS Mutta said he would phone you as soon as it was up and running.'

Angel nodded. Gawber seemed to have all the arrangements in good order.

Angel said, 'There's only Special Operations, you and me know about this gig, Ron. I want to keep it that way. If it leaks out it, it might not work.'

Gawber nodded.

'How are you going to get the super to call a raid?'

'I don't know. That's the next hurdle. I'll have to give that some thought. Got to be very soon.'

* * *

Harker's desk was still loaded with piles of paper. He peered at Angel between two of them.

'What do you want?' he growled.

Angel closed the door and stepped up to him, waving a thin brown paper file.

'Excuse me, sir,' he said, as nonchalantly as he could summon. 'I just wanted your approval to shred this file on Gloria Swithenbank.'

Harker frowned. His forehead was hooded over like an African buzzard.

'Who? Oh, her. Why? It's nothing to do with me. It's DCI Gardiner's baby.'

'Right,' he said and turned back to the door. 'I'll shred it then.'

'Why bother me?'

'The DCI said that she was clean, sir. I had supposed that you had agreed with his findings.'

Harker's pupils flitted rapidly to the right, to the left and then back to the middle of his sockets again. He licked his thin, blue lips.

'What do you mean?' he said suspiciously.

Angel knew he'd roused his curiosity. He'd got him worried. That was good. 'Shredding' had become a dirty word in police stations ever since that trouble in the Humberside force a few years back.

'You know I only want to do what you want, sir. I wouldn't want to have these notes hanging about for anyone to see. There is enough rubbish in the station as it is,' he said, nodding towards the papers on his desk. 'Right, I will shred them.'

Harker pulled an impatient face.

'No,' he suddenly replied.

'All right. I'll leave them here with you to look at then, sir, shall I?' he said, placing them on the pile of papers nearest to him on the desk.

'No. No!' Harker roared. His bloodshot eyes glared at him. He snatched the file and opened it. 'Don't you think I've enough stuff to plough through? What is it?'

'It's on the cover, sir.'

Harker closed the file and looked at the cover.

It read: *Search of the domestic premises of Mrs Gloria Swithenbank, 26 Edmondson's Avenue, Bromersley on 22 March led by DCI Gardiner.*

Harker said, 'Yes. Yes. Well, all this will be in DCI Gardiner's report, won't it? We don't need duplication.' He opened the file again and began to glance down it.

'Yes, sir,' Angel said. 'Pretty much. Except for the conclusion. If you remember, his report said that there was no evidence of the presence of any drugs and that the "intelligence" was duff, whereas I said that although no actual drugs or excess cash were found, I said that the positive behaviour of the sniffer dog could not be ignored. And furthermore, I said to DCI Gardiner at the time, in front of seven other members of the force, that it was obvious to me that Gloria Swithenbank had been tipped off.'

Harker looked up at him. He looked genuinely shocked. His mouth dropped open and he dived into the file.

'You didn't report this to me,' he muttered, his nose still in the report. 'I didn't know anything about this,' he lied.

'You've signed it at the bottom on the last page, page three, and dated it the twenty-sixth.'

He rapidly turned over the page, saw his signature and checked the date. His eyebrows shot up.

Angel had a silent chuckle. He recalled most clearly discussing this with him, but he had not been receptive at the time, and obviously hadn't read the report even though he had signed it.

'All I need to know, sir, is what to do with this file,' Angel persisted slyly. 'If I shred it, nobody need ever know that you had overlooked it.'

Harker's eyes flashed. The skin on the backs of his bony hands tightened. He wasn't falling into that trap.

'Don't come the smart arse with me!'

Angel licked his bottom lip. Maybe he had pressed the point a bit too soon.

'I don't know what your game is,' Harker continued, 'but I have not overlooked *anything*. In fact, I think we should call another search there as soon as possible.'

Just what Angel had wanted. That was great, but he didn't want to let Harker notice he'd been led by the snout.

'There's no need for that, sir. I didn't mean to—'

'No. No,' Harker insisted. He stood up, rubbed his bony chin for a few moments, looked up at the clock then back at Angel. 'In fact, right now,' he added, no doubt believing that he would catch everybody unprepared, especially Angel.

'There's no need,' Angel said, pretending to protest.

'I'll get DCI Gardiner to summon the same team as before,' Harker said pompously. 'That'll include *you*. He can do the warrant. You can leave just as soon as he can get a dog and handler here from Wakefield. Shouldn't take more than half an hour to set up,' he added, reaching out for the phone.

'Right, sir,' Angel said, and left the office.

He smiled all the way up the corridor.

Gawber was in Angel's office waiting for him. He could tell from his face that the trick had worked.

'He's calling DCI Gardiner to assemble a raiding party *now*,' Angel said. 'You've given DS Mutta a photo of Gloria Swithenbank, haven't you?'

'Yes.'

'Well, phone him and tell him to expect her in shot in the next few minutes. I don't want *any* slip-ups!'

* * *

Thirty-five minutes later, two unmarked police cars came down Edmondson's Avenue, while the ARV and the dog handler's van came up it. They stopped at the landmark letterbox outside number twenty-six.

Everything happened almost exactly as before. When they gained access, everywhere was spotless and tidy. Gloria Swithenbank and her mother were sat as cool as cucumbers in the sitting room when the raiding party arrived.

Angel was again paired with Sergeant Galbraith, and he went through the motions of searching the upstairs as before. Of course, nothing was found, the dog was similarly animated in the kitchen area, but even after DCI Gardiner had instructed the constables to lift two floorboards, no drugs or excess cash were found.

The squad left two hours later, more embarrassed than before.

This time, as the police filed out of the house, Gloria Swithenbank was very truculent. She stood on the front doorstep with her arms folded, yelling some of the foulest language after them that Angel had heard from a woman in a long time.

As he drove the BMW away from the front of the house, he cast a sly glance upward at the telegraph pole on the opposite side of the road. A warm, satisfied glow came over him. It was a similar feeling he had had when he heard the judge in a recent case of his sentence a particularly horrible villain — whom Angel had had great difficulty in bringing to trial for murdering two pretty young showgirls after abusing them in a most horrid way — to twenty years' imprisonment.

And Gloria Swithenbank's foul mouth didn't worry him one jot.

THIRTEEN

Although it had gone five o'clock, Angel dashed back to the station to the quiet and privacy of his office. He closed the door, snatched up the phone and dialled a number.

'Hello. Is that DS Mutta?'

'Yes, sir.'

'Angel here. Did the mark, Gloria Swithenbank, show at all this afternoon, Sergeant?'

'Yes, sir. She posted two long flat packets at 15.33 hours exactly.'

'Ah! Good,' he said, breathing a sigh of relief. 'Now, sometime before the official clearance time of 12.45 hours tomorrow, you should see someone unlock the letterbox and retrieve them.'

'Right, sir. I'll be watching out for them.'

'Good man. I shall want blown-up stills of both people providing ID positive enough to make a case to take to court. All right?'

'Got it, sir.'

* * *

Harker was seated at his desk, which was still a mass of paper. He had an opened bottle of Gaviscon in one hand and a screw cap in the other.

At that moment, Angel knocked on the office door.

Harker glanced at the door and curled up a lip. Then he took a quick swig of the medicine, swallowed it, made a face like a marathon runner with a nail in his shoe and hastily screwed the top back on the bottle.

'Come in,' he yelled, as he stuffed the medicine clumsily into an overfull desk drawer and had to struggle several times before he managed to push it down to close it.

Angel came in carrying a videotape and two nine- by six-inch photographs.

Harker looked up at him with a face like an undertaker at a pauper's funeral and snarled, 'Oh. It's you. What have you got there?'

'Good morning, sir,' Angel said brightly.

'There's not a lot good about it. What do you want? I heard from the DCI that the raid on Gloria Swithenbank's yesterday was fruitless. I don't know why I listen to you, really I don't.'

Angel was momentarily speechless. He dismissed the idea of arguing with him, considering the firm, new evidence he was carrying. 'I referred yesterday to the previous raid on Gloria Swithenbank's, sir,' Angel said.

'Yes. You said that you thought that someone had warned her of the raid, also that the dog had been quite animated at one place in the kitchen and may have sniffed out a trace of Class A.'

'Yes, sir.'

'And then you said you were amazed that DCI Gardiner had chosen to ignore these facts. I must say, I would have had to agree with the DCI: they do seem to be rather . . . insubstantial.'

Angel's jaw stiffened.

'They weren't insubstantial, sir. The same thing happened yesterday. Someone had tipped her off. She was expecting us and was well prepared for the raid. She was tipped off by phone by someone from this station.'

Harker pursed his lips and shook his head.

'I rather doubt it,' he said superciliously.

Angel continued, 'In anticipation of that, sir, I had an SE team set up a CCTV camera on the Royal Mail letterbox outside her house. As expected, on hearing by phone from an accomplice that her house was up for another raid, she stuffed the drugs and the cash into prepared bags and went out to her front gate and obligingly posted them into the box. It was done as calmly and as smoothly as if she was posting a piece of wedding cake to a distant friend. I have film and a still of that. Ten minutes or so later, the raid took place and of course her house was free of drugs and again the sniffer dog found only a trace. At six-fifteen this morning, her accomplice unlocked the letterbox with a key, retrieved the packages and walked away. I have got film and a still photograph of that too.'

Harker leaned back in his chair with his mouth open wide enough to catch a swarm of flies.

Angel continued, '*That* also explains the two assaults on the postmen and clears up both those incidents. The first assault was out in the country. In that instance, the villain only wanted a key to the letterboxes. The same key fits all the Royal Mail letterboxes in the district. That's why the postman's keys were reported missing and yet turned up in the gutter the following day. Simply to steal the keys and not let them turn up might have created suspicion. The villain only wanted them to take an impression of the appropriate key to get one made.'

'Ah well, what about the assault in broad daylight on Earl Street?'

'Yes, sir. I'm coming to that. That was the day we searched Gloria Swithenbank's house the first time. The letterbox outside her house on Edmondson's Avenue is due to be cleared each weekday at 12.45. After the tip-off, as before, she would have posted her packages of heroin and cash in the letterbox before we arrived, but on this occasion, because of the timing, the official collection by the Royal Mail van had cleared the box before the accomplice could retrieve the packages. So he had to recover the packages from the collection van sometime before the postman arrived at the end of his run at the sorting office, or the stuff would have been found. The villain knew the route and the timings and caught up with the van on Earl Street. That's where he had actually to steal the van and take it away so that he could search through the mailbags to find the one containing the packages of heroin and cash.'

There was a pause.

Harker looked stunned.

'And where is the heroin and cash now?'

'Don't know for a fact, sir. But he's not had much time to dump it anywhere safely. It could be in his desk or even at his home, but I expect it will be in the boot of his car.'

'And you say you have clear VT of him?'

'Yes, sir. And blown-up stills.'

'Let me see.'

Angel passed the photographs over.

Harker looked at them.

'Aye. She looks a right hard bitch. Gloria Swithenbank?'

'Yes, sir.'

Then he saw the photograph of the man. His jaw dropped.

'It's Galbraith.'

* * *

As soon as Harker had seen the videotape evidence, he summoned Sergeant Galbraith to his office. Angel was required to stay there as a witness.

The sergeant came in looking very smart, professional and innocent. Harker accused him of being in possession and dealing in Class A drugs and outlined the evidence against him. Galbraith didn't reply or offer any explanation. DCI Gardiner and DI Angel immediately searched his desk and car in his presence; four kilos of heroin and more than £8,000 in cash were found still wrapped as seen in the VT, under a rug in his car boot.

Harker told him that he was under arrest, appointed two PCs to guard him, demanded his warrant card, then formally charged him. All Galbraith said in reply was, 'No comment.' And he asked permission to phone his solicitor, and specified Carl Messenger. The superintendent was obliged to give him permission to use the phone and Galbraith made the call. He told Messenger the nature of the charges and that Angel had been the arresting officer.

Then two PCs took him out to be processed and put him in a cell.

Harker then told DCI Gardiner to take a couple of officers to arrest Gloria Swithenbank. He went out of the office.

Angel stood up and made to leave, but Harker waved him down to stay. Angel thought it must be so that he had a witness that he was going through the procedure according to the book.

The superintendent phoned the chief constable, who asked a few questions then rang off. A few minutes later, the chief phoned back to say that he had notified the Professional Standards Directorate, the PSD, and that they were sending an investigating team almost immediately and that they could be expected to arrive at Bromersley station late that afternoon.

Angel then asked if there was anything else he could do and Harker told him that he could leave.

Relieved, he closed the superintendent's door and dragged himself up the corridor to his own office.

WPC Baverstock and DC Scrivens were rushing down with solemn faces. They would be dashing out to the car to join DCI Gardiner to arrest Gloria Swithenbank.

'Congratulations, sir. Great job,' they said as they passed.

He waved an acknowledgement but didn't feel as if he'd earned their plaudits.

He was thinking that when the PSD arrived later that afternoon, Galbraith would be transferred promptly to another police station, and that that would very likely be the last he would see of him until the case was brought to court.

He arrived at his office and closed the door. He was glad to have his own office. He slumped down in the chair and sighed. It wasn't pleasant to see a fellow policeman go down. Galbraith had seemed to be such an honest, dependable sort. But the high-flying system had beaten him. He had succumbed to the temptation of big money and had thought he was too smart to be caught. Angel thought that the station would be rather subdued for the remainder of that Friday; any discussion about the case would be conducted in low voices, and the force would assume an air of shock and mourning for a few days rather than any thought that Galbraith had been behaving in a deceitful and disloyal way, pocketing big money, and spreading the dangerous drug among people of all ages, particularly the young. Loyalty didn't die easily among policemen. However, anger would certainly build against Galbraith when the case was heard in court and the police began to feel the backlash from the public as the media reported the case. Nevertheless, Angel wasn't happy that he had had to be the one to expose a bent copper, even though it had to be done. It therefore took him some time to settle down to any kind of proper work that afternoon. He had gone through the post automatically, emptying envelopes, fastening all the contents of each one with a paper clip and disposing of the envelope in the wastepaper basket, which was an unchallenging job he could manage until he could put himself to matters of a more demanding nature.

A few minutes later, he was better able to apply himself to the work in hand.

There were several unsolved cases he was dealing with; his most important one, of course, was the murder of Joshua Gumme. One of his suspects was Alexander Spitzer, and one of the details concerning him was how he had arrived at The Feathers. Did he have his own transport? He doubted that he would have arrived there on foot. He would have been pretty conspicuous if he had walked through Bromersley town dressed as a priest. He considered that, if he hadn't walked, had he hired a taxi? Or did he have a local friend or contact? Of course, Galbraith could have been the contact. Galbraith had to get his supply of heroin from somewhere. And it was no doubt Spitzer.

Angel also had no idea where Spitzer had come from. The reason why Spitzer and Coulson were still free was because nobody knew where they now lived. They had to have a place they could call their own somewhere. They were too smart to be followed to it. All the time they had been on the run, nobody knew where they were actually running to.

Also, it would be really useful if he knew where Gumme had actually been murdered. At the moment, there was no proper crime scene. You couldn't have a crime scene at the bottom of a river.

His train of thought was disturbed by a knock at the door.

'Come in.'

The door opened. It was Crisp, smiling like a new moon.

'I hear you got Vincent Galbraith for possession and dealing, sir.'

'Yes,' Angel grunted.

'Congratulations, sir. And you got that woman for possession and dealing, too.'

Angel wrinkled his nose.

'Come in, Crisp. Come in. Shut the door. You needn't go on. It's not exactly the crime of the century.'

Crisp blinked. The smile vanished. He closed the door.

'What did you want, anyway?' Angel said.

'You asked me to make enquiries about Gumme's ability to walk, sir.'

'Oh yes,' he said. He had forgotten about it with so much happening. 'What have you got?'

'I saw his GP and he said that Gumme had had a back injury, years ago. He had never seen him walk. He had over recent years prescribed drugs to combat arthritic pain, but he said that he thought he was in pretty good health otherwise. He referred me to a specialist at the hospital who said he had examined Joshua Gumme recently. He had been complaining of pain in the lower back. At the time he agreed with the GP's prescription of painkillers and he said that the nervous system below the waist was so badly damaged that he would definitely not be able to support himself in a standing position. Also, his opinion was that as his wrists and hands were so out of shape and painful with arthritis, he must rule out the possibility of him being able to use crutches. He did say that the rest of him seemed very sound for a man of his age.'

Angel rubbed his chin.

There was another knock on the door.

'Come in, Angel called.

It was Gawber.

Angel looked up.

'Come in, Ron.'

He glanced across at Crisp and nodded. He smiled back.

Gawber closed the door and said, 'Congratulations, sir. So it *was* Vince Galbraith? Pity. I thought he was destined for the top. The obbo idea worked a treat, and you were dead right about the letterbox being used as an emergency hid-ey-hole, and you told me the time of the first raid on Gloria Swithenbank's place that someone must have tipped her off. Pity the DCI didn't act on it.'

Angel smiled and shrugged. He was beginning to recon-cile himself to the morning's events.

'Did you want something else, Ron?'

'You wanted all I could get on the Taskers, sir. I haven't got much. There's nothing at all on either of them on the NPC. James Tasker was assistant manager at the Bromersley Building Society and was doing very well, until it was taken over by the Northern Bank. They made an opening for him at their Todmorden branch, but he wouldn't move so he put himself out of work. His parents are alive and live in Sheffield. They're not known to us. Mrs Tasker was an actress, pretty successful, made two films, did a bit on the telly. Seemed to give it all up for marriage and children. Known by her maiden name Muriel Fitzwilliam. Couldn't find her parents.'

'I remember her . . . Muriel Fitzwilliam,' Crisp said. 'Beautiful she was. Absolutely marvellous. She was in a film about a man, her husband, who was madly in love with her but he was an inveterate gambler. Then there was another man. She fancied him, so, although she loved her husband, she shot him to run off with this other chap.'

Gawber smiled across at Crisp.

'Did you say she *shot* him?' Angel said. And he wasn't smiling.

'Yes, sir. But it was only a film . . . a story. At the Odeon. Yes, sir. And with the new bloke, together they pushed him off the edge of the cliff into the sea. Can't remember what they called it. That new American film star was in it with her . . . Carnegie Jones. He was the one who got her the gun.'

Angel squeezed the lobe of his ear between finger and thumb.

'Interesting,' he said thoughtfully.

Gawber and Crisp exchanged glances.

'It was only a film, sir.'

'Yes. Yes. I know. I understand that.'

'I wish I could remember the name of it.'

Angel suddenly said, 'It's significant that it would take the minimum of two people to hoist Gumme's dead body up and over the rail on Town End Bridge and into the river. That railing is four foot nine.'

'What did Gumme weigh?'

'Eleven stone, two pounds.'

Angel turned to Crisp.

'Whoever shot him had to move him to the bridge. I want you to find out how Spitzer disguised as that priest got to The Feathers, the afternoon of that same night.'

FOURTEEN

It was almost 12.30, Angel's lunchtime. It had been such a dreadful morning that he thought he would like to get out of the office for a brief time. Shake off the atmosphere of distrust and betrayal, and the necessary unhappy business of finding and delivering evidence against a colleague. There are times when unpleasant decisions and actions had to be faced in the police service; there were times when you had to be strong and be seen to be strong. This was one of those days.

He drove the car the short distance to The Fat Duck, parked in the car park and went inside. He was only in there about twenty minutes. He enjoyed a meat pie and two glasses of Old Peculier, gave a heavy sigh, said 'Cheerio' to the landlord and went out into the car park. He made his way to the BMW. There was going to be a lot of tidying up to do in relation to Galbraith and he must return to the office and get on with it. He turned the ignition key and the car burst into life. He engaged first gear and glanced up into the rear mirror. Something white with coloured printing was flapping over the rear window, covering about half of it. He frowned.

Peered more closely into the mirror. It looked like a paper or plastic bag. Strange. It wasn't windy. He didn't think it could have blown there. His lips pulled tight back against his teeth. He knocked the gear-stick back into neutral and got out of the car. He went round the back and discovered that a Tesco plastic bag had been apparently fastened to the window with a couple of pieces of sticky tape. Obviously, it was no freak of the weather. He snatched at the bag, removed it and looked inside; it was empty. He peeled off the bits of sticky tape, rolled up the debris and looked round for a rubbish bin to dump it in. He spotted a small waste basket fastened to a wall by the pub entrance twelve yards away. He went over to it and dropped it in. Then he returned to his car, pulled open the door and looked straight down the barrel of a Megastar semi-automatic pistol. It was in the hand of a man with a long face, tight smiling mouth and small eyes in dark sockets. He was wearing a black raincoat and hat and was sitting in the passenger seat.

Angel gasped. His heart raced.

'Get in,' the stranger snarled.

He wasn't a stranger for long. Angel recognized him from Records. It was Luke Coulson, drug dealer, murderer and long-time associate of Alexander Spitzer.

Angel stood frozen to the spot.

Then he felt the cold, heavy prod of another gun in his left kidney, and a higher-pitched voice with an Irish lilt, from behind, said, 'Get in.'

That voice was even more frightening. He knew it belonged to Alexander Spitzer himself.

He was turning to look, but he saw Coulson slide the safety catch off the Megastar with his forefinger. He dared not take his eyes off him.

'Get in!' Coulson screamed.

'All right. All right,' Angel said quickly and climbed into the driver's seat, his hands out in front of him. He lowered them slowly onto the steering wheel.

Coulson leaned back into the seat but was still pointing the gun at him.

Angel caught a glance of Spitzer's long coat with the fur trimming and the big hat as he closed his door on him. He noted he wasn't in the priest's garb.

He heard the door behind him open, he felt the car rock slightly and then heard the door close. Spitzer was in the back.

There were two of them.

One was one too many.

'What do you want?' Angel said.

'I'll do the talking,' Coulson snarled.

The man in the back seat coughed slightly, then said with the Irish lilt, 'No. *Oi'll* do the talking.'

Coulson didn't say anything. He just turned a corner of his mouth up.

'Drive, Inspector Angel. Drive,' Spitzer said airily.

'Where to?'

'Anywhere that takes your fancy. I want to talk to you.'

The car engine was still running.

Angel engaged gear and let in the clutch. He decided to drive towards the town centre and try to keep to busy areas. He didn't want to be in a lonely spot with these two.

When he had pulled off the car park and reached the main road, he said, 'Well, what do you want with me?'

'Well you may ask, Inspector. Well you may ask. Do you know I was feeling rather chipper this morning? Wasn't I, Luke?'

'You was, Mr Spitzer. You was, indeed. He was feeling on top of the world, Inspector, you know.'

Spitzer continued, 'I was having for my breakfast, half a grapefruit, some French toast and coffee. Then I got a phone call, don't you know. From a man who knows about these things. And do you know what he told me?'

'No.'

'He said that Vincent Galbraith had been arrested and charged by his workmates of possessing and selling the white stuff. Would you believe it, Inspector Angel? His own kith and kin.'

'Disgraceful,' Coulson said, right on cue. 'I call it. Absolutely disgraceful.'

Angel thought quickly. How could Spitzer and Coulson know about Galbraith so early? *Was there another bent copper in Bromersley nick?* Oh God, no!

'So do you know what I did, Inspector Angel?'

'No.'

'I sent the grapefruit and the toast back and instead I called for a full fry-up. Yes. You know, bacon, egg, sausage, tomato, beans, fried bread and black pudding.'

Coulson said, 'And I had the same. The full heart-attack special. If you're going to go, I say, go with a bang!' He waved the gun around and laughed like a hyena.

'And then I heard that you were the arresting officer, Inspector Angel,' Spitzer said. 'How could you do it, Inspector? A nice man like Vincent Galbraith.'

Angel didn't reply straight away. He was considering the best answer to give.

'It's my job,' he eventually said.

'But that's no sort of an attitude. Ratting on your friends?'

Angel slowed, then stopped at a zebra crossing. People crossed.

'Now you see we have a problem,' Spitzer said.

'But it's not insurmountable,' Coulson said.

'No.'

'Not at all.'

There was another pause.

'How much do you think that videotape is worth, Inspector Angel?' Spitzer said.

He hesitated. He could see where this conversation was going. He was a mouse between two cats.

'Supposing, just supposing, that that videotape and the two photos taken from it disappeared. Puff. Just like that,' Coulson said.

Angel shook his head slightly.

He felt the knock of cold steel against his temple. That was Spitzer with the gun.

'Don't shake your head, Inspector Angel, when we're talking to you. It's rude.'

Angel's grip on the steering wheel tightened. His mouth dried up. He tried to swallow.

'How much do you think?' Coulson said.

Angel began to shake his head again, remembered not to, and stopped.

'It's not possible,' he said. 'The tape is evidence. It'll be in the hands of the PSD, the Professional Standards Directorate by now.'

'Too bloody late!' Coulson shouted, and waved his gun at him.

Angel sucked in air. He couldn't help it. He gripped the wheel tightly. He was angry with himself for flinching. He was determined not to show fear again.

A horn blurted from behind. He looked back at the road. The crossing was clear of pedestrians. He pushed the gear lever into first and pulled away.

'Are you sure?' Spitzer said.

'Yes,' he said. He could hardly change his mind.

There was silence.

They seemed to be considering whether they believed him or not.

He sighed. He had to stop at traffic lights.

Angel saw Coulson look back at Spitzer and nod.

There was a pause. The atmosphere cooled a little.

The lights changed to green.

They were off again. He made his way up the gearbox.

Spitzer said, 'Well, well, well, Inspector Angel. That means there's a vacancy.'

'For an enterprising man who is going places,' Coulson added quickly.

Angel didn't know what to say. He could see which way this conversation was now heading. He couldn't become part of their dirty, crooked schemes, but he didn't want to finish up dead either. He didn't know what to say. He sat in silence.

'I've got some questions,' he heard himself suddenly say. He was surprised. It was as if the voice wasn't his. He must have said it out of habit. It was accompanied by a fluttering in his stomach.

'Yes,' said Spitzer. 'That's good. It shows the man has a healthy interest in longevity, Luke. Fire away, Inspector Angel.'

'*Fire away!*' Coulson repeated. 'Fire away!' He gave that frightening hyena-like laugh again.

Angel knew he would have to word his questions very carefully.

'Mr Spitzer, didn't you meet a Mr Joshua Gumme in the entrance hall lounge at The Feathers Hotel a week last Tuesday night?'

There was a pause, then he said, 'I might have done, Inspector. To be sure, I might have done. What's this got to do with—'

'And you made a business proposition to him?'

'What?' he said in surprise.

'That he turned down?'

'Who told you that?' he asked urgently.

'Nobody. I just guessed.'

'He didn't turn it down,' he snapped indignantly. 'He said he would give it serious consideration.'

Angel reckoned he had got it spot on the first time.

Spitzer thought a moment.

'And did you guess what the proposition was?'

Coulson stiffened.

'I didn't know anything about this, Mr Spitzer,' he suddenly said.

'Shh!' he said to Coulson. 'Did you know what the proposition was, Inspector Angel?'

'I thought it might be to use his snooker hall to market more of your poisonous heroin.'

Suddenly Coulson yelled, 'I knew nothing about this, Mr Spitzer! You didn't tell me. You should have told me. I thought we was partners. I should know what is going on.'

'Shut up, you fool,' Spitzer said. 'Anyway, it isn't true.'

Angel didn't believe him.

'Didn't you say that he would earn two million quid?'

'How on earth did you know that?' Spitzer bawled incredulously with the accent of a Leeds loiner. That was his natural accent. He was born in Leeds. He dropped the theatrical Irish voice when he wasn't thinking about it.

'You wrote it down,' Angel said.

'You wrote it down?' Coulson screamed. 'Never write anything down,' he said heavily. 'I've got a bloody idiot for a partner!'

'On one of those religious tracts you were handing round,' Angel persisted. 'He turned you down, so you shot him and bundled him in the river.'

Angel realized that he had gone too far. He didn't know what to expect from Spitzer. Now he had accused him of murder, he knew he could pull that trigger just as easily as wink. He had a tight pain across his chest. It had been there some time but until now his mind had been too occupied to notice it. Now it hurt just too much to ignore. He started breathing deeply in and out to ease the ache.

After a moment he heard Spitzer snigger.

The snigger was a relief.

'No, Inspector Angel. What a thing to say,' he said calmly. The Irish was back.

Angel sighed.

'Well, what did happen then?' Coulson chivvied.

'Really, Luke. Gumme said he would think about it. That's all.'

'Tell me, Mr Spitzer! Not him!' Coulson shouted, his eyes popping out of his head.

Spitzer ignored him.

'Then we were interrupted by a drunk who had some unfinished business with him . . . that's what he said, anyway. Gumme knew him. Didn't like him. Didn't want to be left alone with him.'

Coulson said, 'Well, I expect you stayed there the night. You had a room there, didn't you? Why didn't you leave the drunk and take Gumme up to your room? You could have worked him over. Persuaded him, you know. You would have, if I had been there.'

'I would have done, but the lift was out of order.'

'You could have walked.'

'I could have walked. Joshua Gumme was in a wheelchair.'

There was silence.

Angel could hear the wheels and cogs in Coulson's little brain, meshing and meeting and spinning round and turning other cogs. He wondered what was going to happen next.

Coulson said, 'He could have gone up on crutches?'

'He didn't have any crutches. Anyway, I left them arguing and went to bed. Never saw Gumme after that.'

'Was the man tall, slim, about thirty and probably in need of a shave?' asked Angel.

He heard Spitzer suck in a breath of surprise.

'By God, Inspector. You're good. You're *very* good. How did you know that?'

'You're talking too much, Mr Spitzer. He knows too much now,' Coulson said urgently.

This was all making wonderful sense to Angel. He was getting closer to discovering who murdered Joshua Gumme every minute. The pain in his chest had gone. If ever he got out of this in one piece he knew exactly what he would do.

'He knows nothing that matters. Now shut up!' Spitzer said. 'I'm still running this show.'

'How did he know that then?' asked Coulson. 'You're losing your grip, Mr Spitzer. We are going to be completely out of Bromersley if you don't keep focused.'

'Shut your mouth.'

'I've changed my mind,' Coulson said. 'I don't want this man in our organization, Mr Spitzer. He's too smart. Let's get him to drive under the arches, by the railway.'

Angel knew the place. It was dark and quiet and out of the way. He didn't fancy being found stone cold in a bloody heap tomorrow morning by a tramp looking for somewhere to doss.

'No,' said Spitzer.

Angel was relieved.

Then everything went quiet.

Angel had driven away from the town centre for two miles. He saw a roundabout and drove all the way round it so that they were travelling back towards Bromersley.

Coulson was playing with his gun like a child with a new toy. Then he started looking over the dashboard in front of him. He looked at the RT fitted under the glove compartment. He suddenly turned the gun round and began to hit the dials with the butt of it, smashing the tuner, volume and wavelength changer and anything else until the red monitor light went out.

Angel wanted to object but he managed to restrain himself.

'I've put the red light out!' he screamed excitedly, then he gave that high-pitched laugh. 'Look, Mr Spitzer. The girls will get no punters tonight. The red light's out.'

Spitzer suddenly said, 'Shut up. I'm thinking.'

Angel began to climb a long steep road on the Doncaster side of the town. There were modern red-brick houses on both sides. It led to Cliff Top Inn, which was the highest point around. At the other side of the peak, the road dropped down steeply for about a mile to the busy Bull Foot roundabout and then a few hundred yards onwards to the lowest point of Bromersley, Town End Bridge.

He had to change down a gear.

Coulson was now investigating the rest of the car, hitting things with the butt of the gun. He banged on the catch of the glove compartment. It dropped open. He fished inside and pulled out a duster, a wad of small evidence bags and a pair of handcuffs.

'Hey, look what I've got, Mr Spitzer,' he said, and waved the handcuffs in his direction.

Angel dreaded to think what bright ideas he might be thinking up.

Spitzer suddenly said, 'Luke. Send for our car. We're dumping this. Tell him to pick us up from the Cliff Top Inn on Doncaster Road now.'

'Yeah,' Coulson said cheerfully. 'About time.' He glanced at Angel with a big toothy smile and reached into his pocket for a mobile phone. He opened it up and tapped in a number; a few moments later he spoke into it. Then he closed the phone. 'It's coming, Mr Spitzer.'

Angel thought this must be the parting of the ways for certain. The fluttering of bats' wings in his stomach increased in speed and intensity.

As they reached Cliff Top Inn, the gradient levelled off and Angel changed up to top gear.

Spitzer said, 'Stop here.'

Angel pulled into the side of the road outside the pub door and glanced ahead at the overview of the town and river below. It might have been a great place for a man with a camera. But that day, it was deserted. There were two cars on the pub car park that he could see, but no pedestrians. The wind was wild and strong and was probably keeping people in their homes.

Angel shook his head as he wondered what they were about to do to him.

'Switch off the engine and give the key to Mr Coulson,' Spitzer said.

Angel turned the key, the engine died. He could then hear the occasional growl of the wind.

He passed the key over to Coulson.

Spitzer got out and bounded round to Coulson's window, his big open coat flapping like the arms of a giant wild bear.

Coulson lowered the window and Spitzer whispered something in his ear. Coulson grinned and nodded.

'The next time I'll see you, Inspector Angel, will be in paradise,' Spitzer hollered, then he turned away and strutted in his black leather boots with two-inch heels straight through the open door into the pub, his coat billowing behind him.

Angel wondered what he meant. He hoped he wasn't going to be shot there and then, in cold blood.

From the front seat, Coulson looked around the outside of the car. There was nobody about.

Angel wondered if he was going to do it now, or drive away somewhere. He licked his dry lips and inhaled and exhaled in small, controlled breaths.

'Get out and wait by the door,' he snapped, waving the Megastar automatic at him.

Coulson also got out of the car, dashed round the front of it and opened the back door. 'Now get in here.'

Angel stood on the pavement and looked around. If there had been somewhere to run and hide, like a forest, or a complex of streets and houses, he might have thought of attempting to escape, but there wasn't. If he couldn't move away and find shelter fast he would have been shot dead, there was no doubt about it. Also, he had earlier noted that Coulson seemed to know exactly how near he could safely venture with the gun without the risk of Angel attempting to wrest it from him. It was a desperate time in Angel's life. He was resigned to obeying the man with the gun and climbed into the back seat of the car.

Coulson said, 'Get hold of the roof handle.'

Angel couldn't understand what he was getting at. He looked at him for an explanation.

'Grab hold of the roof handle,' Coulson bawled. 'Put your hand on the grip.'

Angel reached up, turned the handle down and put his fingers through it.

Coulson, as slick as a magician, whipped the handcuffs from his pocket, snapped one cuff onto Angel's left wrist and the other onto the handle itself, so that Angel was shackled to the car.

Angel looked at the handcuffs and realized the mess he was in.

Coulson grinned, closed the door, stuffed the gun in his pocket, opened the driver's door, checked that the gearstick was in neutral and looked back at him.

'Pleasant trip, you bastard,' Coulson sneered. 'Look out, Paradise, here he comes! I hope I never see you again, *anywhere*.'

He released the handbrake, closed the car door, locked it and stood back on the pavement, watching expectantly.

Angel glared at him, like an animal in a glass cage.

The road ahead was a steep hill down to the busiest road junction in Bromersley, Bull Foot roundabout, where six important roads from Sheffield, Doncaster, Barnsley, Wakefield as well as the town centre and B roads to different parts of the outlying districts of Bromersley crossed. If the car kept to the road all the way down the hill, there were vehicles and buses traversing the roundabout all the time. He must hit something or plough into the island.

Coulson's plan was horrific.

However, the car wasn't moving forward. It rocked slightly in the wind.

Coulson stood on the pavement, his hands in his pockets, for a few moments, looking at the car, the wind blowing his trousers wildly round his legs. He pulled a face and stepped out to the rear of the car and began to push it.

Angel reached over the front seat to see how far he could stretch. He couldn't reach any of the controls. The steering wheel, the horn and the handbrake were out of the question. He could reach the RT but he knew it was dead.

He pulled hard on the roof handle and then grabbed it with both hands and swung with all his weight, but he could not budge it. He tried again and swung on it for longer. He made no impression on it whatsoever. The steel of the handcuff scoured his flesh. He thought he felt the car roll forward. He looked out of the window for confirmation. He was right. He saw Coulson becoming smaller and grinning like a madman as he stood in the road. Angel turned round and looked ahead through the windscreen. He could see houses each side moving towards him and passing each side . . . he could feel the rumble of the wheels . . . the car nose-dropped down . . . he looked ahead at the steep hill, and swallowed . . . there was no traffic about . . . that was a godsend . . . it was a wide road . . . he could feel a vibration through his feet . . . his heart pounded like a sledgehammer as the car gathered speed . . . it was keeping a straight track . . . the road he remembered curved near the bottom to go under a railway bridge . . . the houses were passing at a rapid pace now . . . he saw a woman on the pavement carrying something . . . she stared at the car as it sailed past her at a rapid lick . . . there was nothing he could do . . . he could do nothing but sit there and stare through the windscreen . . . the car bounced unevenly as a wheel hit the kerb . . . it jerked violently and caused the handcuff to bite into his wrist. He reached up for the handle . . . determined to hold onto it, come what may . . . the car grazed a wall . . . it careered off it back into the middle of the road. The gradient of the road steepened . . . the car nose dropped more . . . the car accelerated again . . . it seemed almost in freefall . . . he gasped for air . . . he could see the roundabout traffic ahead . . . travelling to the left . . . he was right up to it

188

. . . the side of a red bus was coming up close like film from a zoom lens . . . it passed . . . he was going to hit a heavy wagon . . . it passed . . . a horn sounded . . . a green removals van . . . more horns . . . squeal of brakes . . . blue 'Keep Left' traffic sign . . . loud rattle from underneath . . . silver car . . . a heavy bang, car juddered, everything shook, something fell on his face . . . then he was up in the air . . . blue sky and clouds . . . sucked his breath away . . . hell of a bang . . . crash of glass . . . something fell across his face . . . hot liquid on his neck . . . more blue sky and clouds . . . hell of a bang . . . another turn . . . and again . . . and again . . . then nothing.

FIFTEEN

Nothing.

The screaming sound of a siren and the revving and clunking of a gear change suddenly came to him out of nothingness. He was on his back, rocking about from side to side. His head was stationary; he felt a solid pad at each side of his neck. The rest of him seemed as tightly bound as an Egyptian mummy. Something covered his nose and mouth, and he could hear a persistent hissing.

He opened one eye and then the other and blinked. He could see a red fire extinguisher fastened to a shiny white roof, and to his right a window with the letters 'ECNALUBMA' stuck on frosted glass.

'He's conscious,' a voice said.

A man in spectacles and a green hat peered over him.

'Two seventy over eighty-four,' somebody said.

Angel's ankle hurt. He tried to change its position. He wriggled it. It hurt. It hurt a lot. He thought he had something heavy on his chest. It was tight. He tried to investigate it, but for some inexplicable reason he couldn't lift his hands. They didn't respond. He wasn't even sure he had any hands.

Another voice he didn't know spoke to him, 'Keep still, Michael. Just breathe deeply . . . That's it . . . You're going to be *all* right.'

He wasn't sure he believed him. He was too tired to care.

He licked his lips and ran his tongue round his dry mouth; it was like licking inside a bag of feathers.

Another man in blue and green floated into his field of vision. He stared into his eyes. He had a hypodermic syringe in his hand. He drifted away.

Angel felt a bee sting on the back of his hand.

His eyes closed.

Back to nothingness.

* * *

It was two o'clock on Sunday afternoon and Angel was sitting out in a chair at the side of the bed, in a single-bed ward at Bromersley General Hospital. His neck was bandaged, his right leg and left wrist were in pots, and he had a few, small, bright red marks on his face.

Two days had passed since he had been cut out of his car among a pile-up of other damaged vehicles at the busy Bull Foot roundabout. He was wrinkling his nose, rubbing his chin and wondering how on earth he could organize his rapid discharge from this sterilized torture camp so that he could return to the civilized world of solving murders.

Mary Angel arrived at the open door. She made a pretty picture. She looked at him, surprised and delighted.

'You're awake? You're out of bed?'

His face lit up. Here was the epitome of civilization, love and comfort.

'You look a *lot* better,' she said, leaning over to give him a kiss.

He smiled.

'Are you managing all right?'

'Of course,' she said, pulling up an upright chair next to him. 'I've been very worried about you, Michael. Everybody has. I am glad to see that you're out of bed, and that they've taken that thing off your neck. And, at last, you seem properly awake.'

'Yes,' he murmured.

'Good. That's great news. Now what did the doctor say?'

He wrinkled his nose and pulled a disagreeable face.

'The usual stuff they push you off with. I think I've got a broken ankle, broken wrist, and a cut wound to the neck. That's all.'

She sighed.

'Tell me. Was anybody else hurt in the . . . crash?' asked Angel.

'Not seriously. A man and a woman were treated for cuts. That's all. Only *you* had to stay in hospital.'

He grunted, then said, 'Find out who they are, will you? Send the woman some flowers and I'll write to them both when I get out of here.'

She touched his hand, smiled and said, 'You were very lucky. I understand that your car somersaulted *three* times.'

He sighed. His hand reached out to hold hers.

'Don't let's talk about it.'

She gripped his hand tight and shook it.

'We'll go away on holiday when you get out of here,' she said.

'Yes, we will,' he said, smiling. 'The Isle of Wight. I've always fancied the Isle of Wight.'

'We will,' she replied.

Angel's face suddenly changed. 'But before that, I have some things I must do.'

Mary looked at him. She knew that look of determination. She smiled wryly and shook her head.

He released the hold on her hand and said, 'Have you a pen and paper?'

'I have a pen, love, but nothing to write on.'

'There's something I must write down before I forget it. It's desperately important. It's to do with Spitzer and Coulson.'

She had no idea who they were, but was pleased to do anything to keep him happy.

'I can nip down to the hospital shop,' she said, standing. 'They'll sell writing pads.'

'That would be great. Thank you, love,' he said, his eyes brightening.

'I won't be long,' she said, dashing off.

He reverted to pulling a face, rubbing his chin and wondering how on earth he could break out of this prison and get home in a dignified fashion when another civilized face showed round the door jamb.

Angel's eyes brightened.

It was Ron Gawber.

'Ah! Come in, Ron. Come in,' he said enthusiastically.

'How are you, sir? Are they looking after you?'

'I'm fine. I'm ready to come home, and back to work. I can easily get round the office with a stick, until they take these pots off.'

Gawber smiled.

'You're not expected back at the station for a month or two, sir.'

193

Angel raised his head. His eyes nearly burned holes through Gawber's coat.

'*A month or two*?!' he bawled. 'A month or two?! Don't you worry. I'll be back next week. I've got things to see to.'

Gawber nodded patiently.

'There's no hurry, sir. The super's taken over your cases personally. He said that it was only right—'

'He's done what?' he exploded.

Gawber just looked at him. He realized too late that what he had said was like waving a red rag to a bull.

'He needn't bother. I can see to them,' Angel said through tight lips. 'Besides, I have got them pretty well solved.'

Gawber's eyes brightened.

'Have you, sir?'

'Yes,' he said quickly and moved on. 'Now, I want you to do something for me, Ron. You don't have to tell anybody about it, either. Just do it. First thing tomorrow morning. I won't get out tomorrow. Maybe Tuesday or Wednesday.'

'Might be a week or two, sir.'

'I can't stay here a week or two!' he yelled.

Gawber nodded, but he wasn't convinced.

Angel quickly continued, 'I want to tell you this before I forget it. Now, you know the only reason why Alexander Spitzer and that lunatic, Luke Coulson, are not locked up is because we don't know . . . nobody knows . . . where they actually live. We can never catch them in the act of committing a crime either. They use hotels occasionally, but only while incognito, like Spitzer in that Roman Catholic Father disguise. But I think he's shot that now. They don't use a car, possibly they don't own one, so we can never set up a trace. Spitzer stole a plane recently to bring a cargo of heroin over here, but we don't know what happened to either the cargo or the plane. I reckon they must have a house, a flat, a caravan or accommodation of some sort somewhere in South Yorkshire, because most of the crimes they've committed are round here, and in Lancashire and in Lincolnshire. They don't employ people as such. They set up small-time dealers who work for themselves and buy the heroin from them. Like Galbraith. They like small fry because they can push them around and keep them scared so that they themselves are not betrayed. They are credited with importing more than ten million pounds sterling of Afghanistan heroin through Spain this year alone, so they must have an enormous stash of money or powder somewhere.'

Gawber nodded. He wondered where all this was leading.

'Now then, last Friday,' Angel continued, 'when Vincent Galbraith was accused of possession and dealing, he asked to be able to phone his solicitor. That was fine, and all according to the book. I was present in the super's room when he made the call, and you'll not be surprised to learn that he rang that oily little rag, Carl Messenger.'

Gawber nodded.

'Well, he represents most of the crooks in the area, doesn't he?'

'Aye, well, that was at about 11.25 a.m. He told Messenger the nature of the charge and he gave my name as the arresting officer. Now Ron, at that moment, it was entirely an internal police matter; the only person outside the station who knew about the arrest of Galbraith and my involvement with him was Carl Messenger. Right?'

Gawber nodded, but the lines on his forehead indicated that he still couldn't see what Angel was driving at.

'An hour later. Sixty minutes after the phone call from Galbraith to Messenger, Alexander Spitzer and Luke Coulson ambushed me on the car park of The Fat Duck and started trying to make a deal with me to free Galbraith.'

Realization dawned on Gawber's face.

'Messenger must have phoned them.'

'Exactly. He is the only person who could have. Now, all you have to do is contact the telephone company, trace the call made from Carl Messenger's office phone shortly after he was called by Galbraith, say five minutes after, at approximately 11.30 a.m. on Friday last, get the address, and there you should have Spitzer's and Coulson's hideout. Then liaise with my old friend DI Waldo White, at the Firearms Special Unit, Wakefield. Get his men to surround the place, wherever it is, and wait for them to show. Easy.'

Gawber's face lit up. It looked great. He wanted to get on with it then and there. Suddenly his face changed. He licked his lips and shook his head.

'What about the super? He's supposed to be dealing with Spitzer and Coulson. I wouldn't want to tread on his toes, sir.'

'*What about the super*?' Angel yelled. 'He's not daft, Ron. If you bring Spitzer and Coulson in, he'll be over the moon. You'd not be the *only* blue-eyed boy at Bromersley nick, you know. Credit would naturally fall on him. It would be showered on him from on high. And not only will our chief constable be purring, but there'll be kudos flying his way from the top brass in Manchester, North Yorkshire and the Lincoln forces, believe me,' he said brightly. 'They've all been after those two villains for years.' Then he added, 'And, if, for some reason, it doesn't work out, you can always say I instructed you to do it.'

Gawber grinned. He couldn't lose. It looked great. He couldn't wait to get back into the office.

'Right, sir.'

Angel beamed.

'Great.'

There was something else.

'By the way, sir,' Gawber began. 'You asked me to find out who took Spitzer to The Feathers late that Tuesday afternoon.'

'Yes?'

'It was quite useful that he was dressed as a priest. Made him sort of conspicuous. I checked round the taxi firms and the ranks at the bus station but nobody saw or heard of him.'

'Can't see Spitzer on a bus, somehow.'

'I went to The Feathers and asked around there. The porter remembers that he brought the priest's case in. But he didn't notice the man who drove the car. Took it out of the boot of an old Mercedes, which was mostly loaded with six-packs of Grolsch, he said. He thought it a big joke pulling a priest's sober black suitcase out of a boot stashed with booze.'

Angel frowned.

'An old Mercedes?'

'Mean anything to you?' Gawber said.

'Somebody mentioned an old Merc to me recently, Ron, I'm sure o' that.'

'It doesn't mean anything to me.'

'I'll think about it, Ron. Now, there's something else on my mind, though. Mmmm. I want you to check on that lift at The Feathers. See if it was working the night Gumme was murdered. If it was *not* working then Gumme couldn't have been murdered there. There would have been too many people around the ground floor. They would have heard a gunshot. And there was no way Spitzer or Tasker could have got Gumme upstairs without people noticing. Also, although a pillow would have helped to silence a gunshot, no pillows are missing, so I am coming round to the conclusion that the murder was not committed in the hotel.'

'But Gumme's Walther, the one the murderer used, was found in a downstairs lavatory cistern.'

'Yes,' Angel said thoughtfully. 'I can't understand that yet.'

'And did you just say that Spitzer *or* Tasker could not have carried Gumme upstairs? Was Tasker at The Feathers the night of the murder, then?'

'Yes, I believe he was. According to Spitzer, a man answering his description interrupted them, was arguing with Gumme and being generally annoying.'

'Can you trust Spitzer?'

'It was the way it came out. It wasn't in answer to a question.'

Mary Angel bustled in, carrying a paper bag. She saw Gawber. He stood up. They exchanged smiles.

'Hello, Ron. Nice of you to come.'

They shook hands.

'Nice to see you, Mrs Angel. He's a *lot* better.'

She nodded and smiled.

'I'd better be off,' he said. 'Leave him to you.' He turned to Angel. 'Anything you want, sir?'

'Yes,' he said gruffly. 'I want Spitzer and Coulson on a plate.'

Gawber smiled knowingly.

'Tell Trevor Crisp I want to see him. And Ahmed.'

'Right, and I'll let you know about the lift, sir.'

'Keep in touch.'

He nodded, turned to Mary, smiled and went out.

'He's a nice man, Michael.'

'Aye.'

'He's a gentleman.'

'He's too soft, but he's the best sergeant I've ever had.'

Mary opened the paper bag.

'Writing pad and a pen,' she announced.

'Ta, love. Put it on the locker. Now come and sit down.'

'I can't stay long. I have been asking the sister about you. She says I can only have another two minutes. You are getting far too excitable and you've got to rest.'

'Bloody cheek. You're my wife. You can stay as long as you want.'

Mary didn't choose to argue.

'Well, sit a minute, anyway,' he said, patting her hand. 'There's something bothering me. I've got a problem. I feel a bit guilty, but it really was unavoidable. Part of this bent copper business involved the daughter of Mrs Buller-Price's friend. Gloria Swithenbank is going to go down for drug charges. I reckon she'll get a custody sentence, first offence, might get twelve months or even two or three years . . . It depends how it comes out in court. Now that's going to leave old Mrs Gladstone, who, in her younger days, used to be Mrs Buller-Price's cleaning lady, managing on her own, and I am not sure how she'll take to it. Now, they are still good friends. Still see each other on trips and social things run at St Olave's. Would you be a darling and ring Mrs Buller-Price, tell her . . . well, you know what to tell her . . . explain it all and ask her if she can make time to look in on the old lady and see if she's all right?'

'Of course I will. I can call on Mrs Gladstone myself, if you want me to?'

Angel shook his head and looked down at the pot on his leg.

'I don't think that would do, love. You might get a really hostile reception. The wife of the copper that locked up her daughter . . . going round bringing tea and sympathy. I'm not sure.'

'All right,' she said with an understanding nod. 'Anything else?'

'Yes. I want some clothes. They cut that new suit off me when I was unconscious. And I want some money, some silver for the phone . . . all you've got.'

While she ferreted in her bag for coins, she said, 'By the way, those cheap playing cards you left on the dressing table . . .'

His ears pricked up. He looked up at her and frowned.

'Yes? What about them.'

'What are they for? I played a game of patience with them. And they're useless.'

'Useless?' he said, his eyebrows shooting up. 'What do you mean, useless? And they're evidence.'

A woman in a blue dress and little white cap came in. She stood with folded arms at the door.

'I'm afraid you'll have to go, Mrs Angel. He's got to have his rest.'

'This is my wife, Sister,' Angel said assertively.

'I know. We've met.'

'I'm coming, Sister,' Mary Angel said.

'Visiting time goes on until six, doesn't it?' Angel said.

The sister didn't reply.

Mary put a pile of silver on the locker top.

'That's all I've got.'

'Ta, love.'

She quickly reached down for her handbag.

Angel's lips tightened. He looked at the sister. 'What's the panic?'

'There's a cup of tea on the way,' the sister replied.

'Goodbye, sweetheart. See you tomorrow.'

She gave him a kiss.

'Take care, love. Oh,' he said. 'Will you wheel me the telephone trolley in?'

'I'll see to it later, Mrs Angel,' Sister said.

Angel pulled a face.

Mary was at the door.

'What about those playing cards?' he called. 'What's the matter with them?'

'They're simply no good, love. Anyway, take care and I'll see you tomorrow.'

'What do you mean they're no good?' he bawled.

It was too late. She had gone.

The sister advanced towards him.

'Come along. Let's get you back into bed,' she said, snatching at the bedding. 'You've been sat out long enough. Stand up. Lean on the chair arm. Keep that foot up. Let's have that dressing gown off.'

Angel's jaw dropped.

She began peeling off a sleeve.

'A young man called Ahmed called in to see you, but I headed him off. You already had two visitors and it's only two visitors to a bed, you know. Told him he can come tomorrow. Now sit on the bed. Take your slipper off.'

Angel's eyes nearly popped out of his head. The pain was too much or she might have heard him describing her in terms of a female in the canine world.

SIXTEEN

The hospital porter sighed and pushed Angel in the wheel-chair out of the lift into the corridor.

'Now, now, sir,' the brown-coated elderly man said, 'we'll soon have you back in bed.'

'I don't want to go to bed. I've been in bed for four days. I've had enough of bed.'

'Well, tomorrow, I expect you'll be having *more* physiotherapy.'

'I don't need any more physiotherapy. I can do all that physio stuff at home . . . better still, in my office. I don't need a little lass to teach me how to walk,' he bawled. 'I have been walking for years! I've got the hang of it now.'

'Well, we're nearly back on your ward. You're going to be all right.'

'I know I'm going to be all right, but I would be a damned sight more all right at home.'

Angel looked up and by the nurses' counter and desk, opposite his ward, was a figure he was very pleased to see.

'There you are, sir,' Gawber said.

Angel's face brightened.

'Hello there. Nice to see you. Come on in, Ron, before Sister Himmler shoves a catheter up you.'

Gawber smiled and followed them into the ward.

The porter pushed the wheelchair up to the side of the bed.

'I'll get a nurse.'

'Don't bother. I can manage,' he called, but the porter had gone.

Angel slowly transferred himself from the wheelchair to the upholstered chair at the side of the bed.

Gawber could see by his contorted, perspiring face that his boss was still in some discomfort.

'Sit down. Sit down,' Angel said irritably. 'Listen, Ron,' he said with a sigh. 'Last night, I suddenly woke up. Don't know why. I hadn't been dreaming or anything, but I woke up and from nowhere, I remembered who had told me about a Mercedes . . . only he called it an "old Merc". It was Ben Johnson. Yes. It was definitely Ben Johnson. He said he had bought it because it was good for pulling girls . . . or something similar. And when I thought about it, I also remembered something else. I remembered seeing him drinking from a can of Grolsch when I interviewed him at the snooker hall.'

Gawber nodded.

'That fits.'

'Yes. And there's something else. Johnson came out of Durham prison in 2004, didn't he? Wasn't Spitzer in Durham in 2004?'

'I'd have to check up on that, sir,' Gawber said, then he grinned. He had a twinkle in his eye.

'I've got some news too, sir,' he said quickly.

Angel realized he had done all the talking and not given him a chance. He could see it was important.

'Aye. What is it? What is it? Spit it out, Ron,' Angel said, full of anticipation.

'I've got Spitzer and Coulson's address,' he said grandly.

'Great stuff.'

'It's a small farmhouse between Wakefield and Huddersfield. It's got a few outbuildings and a couple of barns. Fairly isolated.'

'You got it from the telephone company?'

'It worked. Just as you said, sir.'

'Good. Good. Messenger has no idea you've made the inquiry?'

'No.'

'Great. When are you going in?'

'Six o'clock tomorrow morning.'

Angel bit his lip. He would have given anything to be leading the raid. 'You've set it up with Waldo White?'

'Yes, sir.'

'That's great. Let me know what you find and how you get on.'

Gawber nodded. He noticed that Angel was looking at the fingers peeping out through the pot on his left hand. He moved them slightly.

'Do they hurt?'

'Can't feel them. I wish I could.'

'What's the doctor say?'

He pulled an impatient face.

'They don't know anything,' he said disdainfully. 'Got to wait and see.' He gritted his teeth and said, 'You know, Ron, if I don't recover the full use of my hand, they'll chuck me out of the force.'

Gawber knew that what he said was right; he also knew that it would be devastating to a man like Angel.

'It'll be all right, I expect, sir,' he said encouragingly. Then he wondered what he could say to take Angel's mind off his hand. He was glad that he remembered he had some more news. 'By the way, sir. I almost forgot. I saw the desk clerk at The Feathers and he eventually, reluctantly, admitted that the lift was not working the night of Tuesday, March 20th, the night of the murder.'

Angel's face brightened.

'Ah. I thought so. Well, Ron, that means that Gumme could not have been murdered in The Feathers. He must have been taken from there, sometime later that evening, to another place, where he was shot, then transported in a vehicle, a car presumably, and then hoisted over the bridge wall and dropped into the river.'

'And his wheelchair dropped in after him.'

'Or before him. He was shot with his own gun. I assume he pulled the gun on someone, and that party, man or woman, took the gun from him and shot him.'

'But the gun was found in the gentlemen's loo, in the hotel, sir. I found it. It was wiped clean of prints.'

'Hmm. It doesn't make sense, does it?'

'It would need a deliberate trip back to The Feathers with it . . . at the risk of being seen.'

Angel squeezed the lobe of his ear between his finger and thumb.

'I think the murderer must have brought the gun back to The Feathers deliberately to try to involve Spitzer in the crime. It would have seemed to him or her to be a great idea to take advantage of the presence of a well-known murderer, like Alexander Spitzer, on the scene. And if you knew that Spitzer was actually to meet the intended victim, so much the better. To the murderer, it would have been seen to be like a gift from the gods. But, of course, it didn't go to plan. He didn't count on the unforeseen possibility that the lift would be out of order and that that would prevent Gumme reaching a suitable part of the building where he could have been quietly disposed of.'

Gawber nodded.

'That sounds right, sir. Of course, sir, the gun being found in the gents' loo means that the murderer must have been a man.'

Angel grunted in agreement; his mind was racing.

'So the murderer is someone cunning,' Angel said, 'someone with transport, someone devious enough to try to lay a trail for the police away from himself, towards Spitzer or someone else at the hotel, someone with a criminal mind, been in trouble with the law before, physically strong enough to be able to hoist Gumme up and over the rail on the bridge and into the river, and hates the man enough to want him dead.'

'It's looking like Ben Johnson, sir.'

Angel nodded.

'Yes. He hated being called Bozo. He said so. Maybe he had a secret hatred of Gumme. He said he didn't get any support when he accidentally killed the man in his snooker hall. That's why Gumme charitably gave him a job when nobody would lift a finger to help him.'

'Aye, and maybe it *wasn't* such a charitable deal at all. Maybe Gumme was simply stuck for a glorified lavatory cleaner.'

'Aye,' Angel had to agree. 'There's no big rush for those sort of jobs these days, is there? Well, see if Johnson and Spitzer were in Durham prison at the same time. Then pick him up, PDQ. You'll have to interview him again. Read my notes. I'd like to do it. You'll have to play it very canny. Oh, I wish I was out of here. They're not giving me any treatment. Just pills and a physio lass walking me up and down like an infant for half an hour in the mornings. I can do *that* at home.

If I could only get out of here, Ron, you could take me to the office, I could work from there.'

* * *

Angel was in a wheelchair, fully dressed, except for one shoe, and he had a small suitcase across his lap.

He was beaming and full of bonhomie and anticipation.

'Mr Angel!' Sister bawled as she came into the ward carrying a small paper bag and a letter.

He looked up at her from the wheelchair.

'Now listen very carefully, Mr Angel. In this packet are enough pills for one week, seven days. It's two every six hours of the white ones, day and night. No more than eight in twenty-four hours. Your sleeping pills are the little blue ones . . .'

The bonhomie vanished. He pulled a face like he'd collared a burglar and let a murderer escape.

'I don't need any sleeping pills, Sister.'

'Your sleeping pills are the little blue ones,' she repeated heavily. 'Take one at night. Take them. They will give you a good night's sleep, even if you *think* you don't need them. They are not addictive and will help your recovery.'

Angel shook his head.

'Sister,' he began. 'I don't need any—'

'You must do as I tell you!' *she boomed.*

'You won't be there,' he said impudently.

She stared at him with eyes like Midas.

'It is not yet too late to stop you from going, Mr Angel. I do not entirely approve of this early discharge and I have made Doctor Eisennman aware of my views. He says that there are special reasons why this concession has been permitted; as you have made yourself particularly obnoxious to some of my senior staff, I have waived my objection.'

Angel blinked and was about to reply.

'Now then, to continue,' she said. 'Do the exercises as you've been instructed by the physiotherapist each day. You must certainly not undertake any kind of work or make any journeys in motor vehicles — only the necessary one back to the hospital. Watch your diet. No fatty foods. No sticky cakes. No alcohol. No smoking. Do nothing that would unduly increase your blood pressure.'

'You mean no—'

'You may ring the telephone number,' she boomed, 'at the top of the letter, if you have any medical difficulty or are in any additional pain. You may borrow the wheelchair but it must be returned. I understand that there is a person waiting with a car at the main door to take you home. A porter has arrived to wheel you down there and Student Nurse Plimpton here will assist you into the car. You have an appointment with Doctor Eisennman in outpatients next Wednesday. Full instructions are on the letter. *Don't miss it*. Any questions?'

'Will you be there?'

'No.'

'I won't miss it.'

* * *

Ahmed led the way up the green corridor, carrying the suitcase.

Half a dozen heads shot out of the CID room, and took in the unusual sight of Angel in a wheelchair, with pots on his foot and hand and places on his face that were already turning from dark red to an uninteresting pink, being pushed up the corridor by Crisp.

They called, 'Well done, sir,' 'Welcome back,' 'Great job, sir.'

Angel smiled and waved with his right hand. The hand in a pot rested unresponsively on the wheelchair arm.

Ahmed opened the office door, rushed in, deposited the case by the wall, then pushed the swivel chair out of the way into the corner, as Crisp wheeled Angel up to the desk and then squared him up to face it.

'Ah,' Angel said, with a grin. 'That's better. Thank you, son.'

Crisp nodded and made for the door.

'Where are *you* going?'

'Got a lot on, sir.'

'Like what?'

'Investigating a burglary, sir. A garden hut on Creeford Road. I am in the middle of enquiries about a stolen bicycle, a lawnmower and fourteen pounds of rabbit food stolen from—'

'Oh. You can leave that, son,' he said positively. 'You can definitely leave that.'

Crisp's mouth opened. He wasn't too pleased. He came back up to the desk.

Angel glanced at the pile of post, notes and round robins that had accumulated in his short absence, then he looked up at Ahmed.

'A cup of tea would go down a treat.'

Ahmed smiled. 'The kettle's been on, sir.'

'Right. Chop-chop, then,' he said and gestured towards the door.

Ahmed rushed out.

Angel looked up at Crisp.

'Now, I know that Ron is busily tied up with something, so I want you to find out if Benjamin Johnson and Alexander

Spitzer were in Durham prison at the same time. Johnson was in from 2000 and was released in January 2004. Spitzer also served time there, but I want you to find out exactly when he was there, sharpish.'

Crisp nodded and went out.

Angel took the phone off its cradle and laid it on the desk. He tapped in a number and then picked it up. He could hear the number ringing out and eventually it was answered by his wife, Mary.

'Hello,' she said.

'It's me,' he said, smiling.

'Where are you?' she said.

'At the station. Are you all right?'

'Yes. You crafty old fox. How did you manage that?'

'It's a long, long story. But I'll be home for tea. I'll get a lift from one of the lads.'

Mary Angel must have smiled. 'You must have really got right up that poor sister's nose.'

'Not at all,' he said with a chuckle. 'I was Mr Charm personified. Now about those playing cards?'

'I'll have to get something defrosted very quickly,' Mary said, sounding her usual, considerate, domestic self. 'I don't know what we can have. You could have told me. Are you on any special diet? Is there anything you *can't* have?'

'No,' he said. 'No restrictions at all. I can have anything I like. You'll find something,' he said knowingly. 'About those playing cards?'

'I've got some lamb chops. They should be all right. They looked very nice. I'll have to move fast. Let me go now, Michael, or you won't be having tea, it'll be supper.'

There was a knock at the door.

'Come in,' he called.

It was Ahmed with a tin tray with a cup and saucer in the middle of it.

'All right, love. I'll see you about a quarter past five.'

'Bye.'

He replaced the phone.

Ahmed put the tea on the desk in front of him and said, 'Have you heard the news, sir?'

'No. What?'

'You'll be pleased, sir,' he said, his eyes shining. 'The super's arrested Alexander Spitzer and Luke Coulson. They're down in our cells, here, now.'

Angel nodded.

'I knew Ron Gawber was organizing a raid on their farm-house.' Then he sniffed. 'Did you say the *super* had made the arrest? Where was DS Gawber?'

'Oh, he was *there*, sir, and there was an armed unit from Wakefield as well.'

'Any casualties?'

'No, sir. They went in early doors, caught them unawares.'

Angel smiled quietly and sipped the tea. 'Did they find anything . . . incriminating on the . . . premises?'

'Huge store of heroin, sir. Suitcases of money. There was even an aeroplane hidden under straw in a barn.'

Angel nodded, sipped the tea again and then held the cup thoughtfully and said, 'Has the PSD team moved Sergeant Galbraith out of our cells?'

'What's that, sir?'

'The Professional Standards Directorate. PSD. Time you knew these abbreviations.'

'Oh yes, sir. They came on Friday. Started taking statements from everybody, and they took the Sarge away with them then. Don't know where.'

'They wouldn't have told you if you had asked,' he said starkly.

The reason he had asked was that he hadn't wanted Spitzer and Coulson to learn they were sharing a cellblock that had a bent copper in it. Bromersley force would never have heard the end of it.

Ahmed nodded his understanding.

'Ron will be busy processing Spitzer and Coulson and interviewing them, then?'

'Yes, sir, with the super. Do you want to go down? I'll wheel you down there if you want me to.'

He wrinkled his nose.

'No. No. They're old hands. They'll be singing "No comment" to every question. It would be a waste of time. Besides, there are charges they have to answer, not just here, but in Manchester, York and Lincoln that I know of. And there'll be others I don't know of. That'll keep Ron and the super and the CPS busy for long enough.' He shook his head determinedly. 'No, Ahmed, I have enough on my plate. I've got a murder to solve.'

The phone rang. He reached out for it.

'Angel.'

It was Crisp calling from the CID office.

'Spitzer was in Durham prison from July 20th 1997 to April 22nd 2004. Johnson was in Durham prison from February 22nd 2000 to January 10th 2004. So there was an overlap time of almost four years. They didn't share a cell, but they were in the same wing and on the same landing.'

'Ah,' Angel said eagerly. 'Then they would certainly know each other. Right, now go to the snooker hall on Duke Street and ask Mr Benjamin Johnson if he would kindly accompany you back to the station to see me. And be nice, Crisp,' he said gently, then his jaw stiffened and he added, 'But don't come back without him.'

An hour later, Crisp wheeled Angel into Interview Room One where Benjamin 'Bozo' Johnson was already seated with his solicitor, a smartly dressed young man. Their eyebrows lifted slightly as they took in the unusual sight of a police inspector being pushed into the room in a wheelchair, but they said nothing.

Crisp switched on the recording tape.

Angel began quickly in a monotone, 'Interview Tuesday April 3rd at 12.45 p.m. Present, Benjamin Johnson, Mark Walker, Detective Sergeant Trevor Crisp and Detective Inspector Michael Angel.'

He turned immediately to Johnson.

'Where were you during the late afternoon, about five o'clock on Tuesday, 20th March last?'

He frowned, touched his nose with his forefinger and said, 'Five o'clock? I would be at the snooker hall on Duke Street.'

Angel sniffed.

'If you've forgotten, that was the day Joshua Gumme was murdered.'

Johnson didn't even blink.

'Yes. I was at the snooker hall. I'm almost always there.'

'Are you the owner of a 1994 Mercedes car? Silver with a red stripe down the side?'

'Yes. That's my car.'

'Do you ever lend your car out to anyone, to a friend, or hire it out to anybody?'

'No,' he said firmly.

'Has it ever been stolen?'

'No,' he said. 'What are you getting at, Inspector?'

Angel was glad he had asked. It might save time. He made a leap in the dark with his next assertion.

'Your car was used to transport a man dressed as a priest, but who was actually a wanted murderer and drug dealer, Alexander Spitzer, to The Feathers Hotel at around five o'clock that day. Are you saying you *weren't* the driver?'

'Oh? That?' Johnson said, wrinkling his nose, looking down at his navel and then at a white splash left by a bird on a windowpane. 'That? No. I drove him to the hotel.'

'Why didn't you say so?' Angel said tersely.

'I had forgotten it was the same day.'

'Why? How many times have you driven a man dressed as a priest to The Feathers Hotel?'

Johnson knew he'd been exposed.

'I didn't realize it was the same day, that's all.'

Angel shook his head impatiently. He turned to the solicitor. 'Mr Walker, you should advise your client not to lie unless it's absolutely necessary.'

'He wasn't lying. My client had obviously forgotten, that's all.'

'Well, I hope he doesn't *forget* anything else I ask him about. The questions are going to get more significant as we move on. Now then, Mr Johnson, how did you come to be taxiing murderer and drug dealer Alexander Spitzer around the place?'

'It was only the one time. I met him off a train in Doncaster and brought him to The Feathers, that's all. He knew I worked for Mr Gumme. He asked me all about him. I didn't know much. I think he thought I could put a word in for him regarding some business he wanted to put to him. I couldn't, of course. The boss wouldn't have listened to me.'

'Why did he choose you?'

'I don't know.'

Angel wrinkled his nose. He turned to Walker and said, 'Will you give him a kick or something? His memory's on the blink again. It might need a six-pack of Grolsch to get it started.'

Walker leaned over and whispered in Johnson's ear.

Johnson frowned, turned to Angel and said, 'You mean why did Spitzer get me to taxi him?'

Angel made an exaggerated smile, nodded and said, 'Yes.'

'I knew him from the time I was in Durham prison.'

'You were on the same landing for four years,' Angel said forcefully. 'You couldn't avoid knowing him. How well did you know him?'

'He was top dog. Practically ran the wing. Bossed all the rackets.'

'So you were scared of him?'

'*Everybody* was scared of him.'

'So he got in touch with you and asked you to meet him in Doncaster and taxi him to the hotel.'

'Yes.'

'And what else?'

'What else? Nothing else.'

'Didn't he ask you to stick around in case he needed your assistance with something?'

'He might have done.'

'Of course he did. Or else he was slipping. What else did you do for him? Did you take him and Gumme for a drive in your car to have a natter, seeing as he couldn't get to talk to him privately at the hotel?'

'No.'

'And didn't Gumme lose his patience with Spitzer, pull out his gun in an attempt to get away from him and you?'

'No.'

'And didn't Spitzer take it from him, shoot him and then the two of you went to Town End Bridge to throw his dead body and his wheelchair off it, into the River Don?'

'No.'

'You were Spitzer's accomplice and therefore complicit in the offence of murder.'

'No. No. I was at the snooker club. I was there *all* evening. Every minute.'

'Any witnesses?'

'No one in particular I can think of, but I was *there*. I guess some of the punters would remember me.'

'Could Horace Makepiece confirm you were there?'

'Well, no. Not exactly. He was . . . in and out.'

'What time did Makepiece arrive?'

'I told you that before, he got back at about eight-fifteen.'

'Did you see him come in?'

'No. He went to the printing room; he was printing up some menus for the Chinese or something.'

'So how did you know he got back at eight-fifteen?' Angel bawled impatiently.

'He *told* me,' Johnson responded in like fashion.

Angel ran his hand through his hair.

'But you didn't actually see him?'

'No. I was busy. The place was throbbing. All the tables were let. I was on my own. He turned up at about ten-thirty.'

'Has he got a key for the front door?'

'No.'

'But you had emptied the place, and locked up by this time?'

'Yes.'

'Which way did he come in?'

Suddenly Johnson's face dropped.

Angel didn't miss it.

'He came in by the front door, didn't he?' Angel said quickly. 'You had to unlock it to let him in.'

'I didn't think about it.'

Angel's pulse increased. 'So he couldn't have come from the print room?'

'I suppose not.'

'Didn't you think it . . . strange? Particularly as he had made a point of establishing in your mind that he had returned from chauffeuring Mr Gumme at eight-fifteen?'

'Naw,' he said. 'Knowing the boss was at The Feathers, I just thought he'd been at it with Ingrid again, that's all.'

Angel and Crisp exchanged glances.

His solicitor looked at his client and tried to remain expressionless.

Johnson sat there with a dirty grin on his face.

'Well, not so surprising, is it?' he continued. 'The boss wouldn't be that much use to her, paralysed from the waist down. Surprised she chose Harelip though. Poor woman must have been desperate.'

Angel sighed and took the moment to shuffle himself into a more comfortable position in the wheelchair.

At length, he rubbed his chin and said, 'What makes you say that Mrs Gumme and Mr Makepiece might have been "at it"?'

He shrugged.

'He told me. Used to swank about it. There were several men. Everyone knew that that's what had been going on. Except the boss.'

Angel scratched his head.

* * *

Crisp pushed Angel in the wheelchair back up the green corridor to his office and squared him up in front of the desk.

'Crisp,' Angel said. 'Nip out and bring in Horace Makepiece. He should be at the snooker hall on Duke Street. Be quick about it and whatever you do, don't let him speak to Johnson. I don't want those two cooking up their own fairy story. All right?'

'All right, sir.'

'You've got a head start on Benjamin Johnson of five minutes, so crack on.'

'Right, sir,' he said, making for the door.

'And on your way down,' he called, 'tell Ahmed I want him, pronto.'

'Right, sir.'

The door closed.

Angel wriggled uncomfortably in the chair. He arched his back and tried to move the fingers in the pot. They seemed to respond. He couldn't actually see them move, but he thought the tendons tightened in response to his stretching. He tried again. Nothing moved. He wondered if it was merely wishful thinking. He sighed. It was suddenly very quiet. Very quiet. He looked around at the green and yellow walls, the grey metal desk and stationery cupboard, the imitation black leather upholstered swivel chair with its chromium-plated feet, and the striplight in the cream ceiling that some days would flicker. It was the first few quiet moments he had had in the station since that ride of death down Doncaster Hill Road into the bottom of Bull Foot roundabout, then bouncing like a beach ball over the island three times and crashing into a furniture van at the other side. He was so glad and thankful to have come out of it alive and be back here in his own office, solving crimes, seeking out criminals and contributing towards the promotion of equality in an unfair society.

There was a knock at the door.

'Come in.'

It was Ahmed. He looked anxious. He came up to him, looked closely into his face and said, 'Are you all right, sir?'

Angel looked back at him and smiled.

'Yes, Ahmed. I'm fine.' He looked puzzled. 'Will you phone and arrange transport for a witness, Benjamin Johnson, back to Duke Street? He's in Interview Room One. And ask the driver, whoever it is, to take him by the long route.'

Ahmed frowned. 'The long route, sir?'

'Tell them it's for me,' he said. 'They'll know what you mean.'

Ahmed looked puzzled.

'And a cup of tea wouldn't go amiss.'

'Righto, sir, straight away.'

The door closed.

The phone rang. He reached out and picked up the hand-piece.

'Angel.'

'It's DC Scrivens, sir. Great to have you back, by the way.'

'Thank you, Ted. Now, what is it?'

'I'm in reception, sir. There's a young woman here . . . it's a bit odd. She's asking to see you about the Gumme case. She says she knows you. Her name is Mrs Muriel Tasker. Says she wants to make a confession.'

SEVENTEEN

'I broke into the Gummes' house and took back the garnet necklace my husband had bought me,' Muriel Tasker said boldly. 'I had never done anything dishonest in my life. But it was the way it had been taken from me by that monster, Gumme, that so antagonized me that I was determined to get it back. My husband had said that I should let it go, but I am made of stronger stuff. I watched to see her leave in that fancy car of hers, then I broke the back window with something, climbed in through the window, the alarm started ringing but I took no notice of it. I soon found the bedroom. The necklace was on the dressing table. I just grabbed it, ran back to the window and was out in no time. I ran all the way back home. I was exhausted. I have had the necklace back just over a week now. I don't get as much pleasure from it, knowing that that tart had been wearing it.'

She banged it down on the table in front of him.

'There you are. They can't give me long for taking back something that was mine, can they?'

'No,' Angel said. 'Why didn't you drive there and park nearby?'

'We don't have a car, Mr Angel. Gumme didn't leave us anything.'

Suddenly, Angel's eyes glazed over. It was at that moment that he realized who the murderer of Joshua Gumme must be.

'Excuse me, Mrs Tasker. There's something important I must see to. It cannot possibly wait.'

He leaned over, took the phone handpiece off its cradle, put it on the desktop, tapped in a number and then picked it up.

The phone was soon answered.

'Come in here, Ahmed. There's something important I want you to do.'

'Right, sir.'

He replaced the phone.

'Now then, Mrs Tasker, sorry about that. Where were we?'

'Mr Angel, how long do you think I'll get?'

'Oh,' he said pensively. 'First offence . . . your own property . . . probably a fine. It would be up to the judge.'

* * *

'Now then, Mr Makepiece, I'll get straight to the nitty-gritty. Where were you between eight-fifteen and approximately ten-thirty, the night Joshua Gumme was murdered?'

Makepiece licked his lips.

'I told you, Inspector, I was in my little printing room, in the back of the snooker hall. You know. You've been there. I was printing the menus—'

'No, you weren't. Think again.'

Makepiece looked round Interview Room Number One. He looked at his solicitor, then at Crisp and then back at Angel.

'But I *was*,' he insisted. 'I was running Charlie Wong's menus in the printing room.'

'No you weren't. Do you want to go for third time lucky?'

Makepiece licked his lips and swallowed. He didn't say anything.

Angel said, 'You seem to have had a memory lapse. I'll tell you why you couldn't have been in the printing room, shall I?'

Makepiece simply looked at him.

'Because you had to be let in the main door by Bozo Johnson at around half past ten. If you had been in the printing room, you would have already been in the main building.'

Makepiece's eyes bounced. He licked his lips.

Angel said, 'Look, I already know that you were having an affair with Ingrid Gumme. And that's a very strong motive for murder.'

Makepiece groaned in protest. His face went white.

'It wasn't me. It wasn't. I have had no affair with Ingrid Gumme.'

'You weren't in the printing room that evening,' Angel said firmly. 'Do you want to tell me where abouts you were?'

His solicitor leaned over and whispered in his ear.

Makepiece shook his head at him.

'I ain't done nothing. I've got nothing to hide. I ain't going in the pokey for nobody.' He turned to Angel. 'Yes,' he said. 'All right, I'll tell you where I was.'

Angel gestured to him to continue.

'I came to work for Mr Gumme about seven years ago as a driver. He was stuck in a wheelchair even then and had not long been married to Ingrid. When the boss was away, well, the cat used to play. Ingrid always was flighty. She used to wear revealing swimsuits then brush up close to you. She'd run her hands slowly down her body, suggestively, like, and so forth . . . ordinarily, I might have been tempted. I can't pretend I didn't notice or that it had no effect on me. But I know when to keep off the grass, and that was turf I had no intention of playing ball on. She used to say how she fancied me. Me? I ask you. With a face like mine. She kept saying things like how unhappy she was and hinted if the boss died she'd need somebody to help her spend his money. I'm not daft, Inspector. If she's behaving like that and saying stuff like that to an old soldier like me, what on earth is she saying to younger more obliging punters? Anyway, I didn't want no trouble. I was nice and cosy wid the boss and I wanted to keep my job, so I tried to keep my distance from her, widout falling out wid her, if you sees what I mean. Then about ten days ago, Ingrid told me that the boss had said that a big crook called Spitzer wanted to meet him at The Feathers and that he was going along to discuss the idea of maybe dealing a load of heroin in the snooker hall. She said this was the golden opportunity to get rid of the boss and get Spitzer blamed for it. I said that I wanted no part in it. The boss came in so we couldn't talk no more.'

His voice trailed away.

'Then what?' Angel said.

'Well, the night I took him to meet Spitzer at The Feathers, I dropped him off and came back to the boss's house. Put the Bentley quietly in the garage, and dropped the door as I told you. I was going to put the keys through the letterbox as usual, then she appeared through the French window in front of the swimming pool. She wasn't wearing much and she invited me in. I told her that I couldn't do anything to hurt the boss. She made light of it and said that she had only been joking. We had a few drinks and to cut a long story short we went to her bedroom. The first time and the only time. Afterwards, as we got dressed she said would I drive her to The Feathers. It was more of an order than a request from the boss's wife.'

'Oh yes,' Angel said dryly.

'Anyway, I drove her there and then she said the strangest thing. She said she could drive herself back. She said would I mind walking home. Didn't want to keep me up. It was about ten o'clock by now. I said OK.'

Angel said, 'You would, her being the boss's wife.'

'I walked back to the snooker hall, got there about ten-thirty and the rest you know. That's the truth, Mr Angel. The honest gospel truth.'

* * *

'You know who murdered Gumme then, sir?' Crisp asked quietly as he pushed Angel in the wheelchair up the green corridor.

'Oh yes,' Angel said as he nursed his plaster-covered left wrist in his right hand. 'I've instructed Ahmed to brief John Weightman and WPC Baverstock, to get warrants and scramble whatever PCs and vehicles they can to bring them in.'

Crisp's eyebrows shot up.

'You've worked it out then, sir?' he said excitedly, as he opened the office door and pushed the wheelchair up to the desk. He closed the door and then sat down opposite him.

Angel smiled.

'It's easy when you get all the information. Muriel Tasker has just filled in all the missing blanks. Take this garnet

224

necklace of hers. Among other things, she has just told me that her husband, James Tasker, handed it over to Gumme two weeks ago as a contribution to the impossible debt he had incurred. A week later, she admits to breaking into the house and taking it back from Ingrid Gumme's dressing table. Fair enough. But I have to ask myself, how did she know that that's where it would be? Gumme could have sold it, given it to someone else, put it in a safe, taken it to the jewellers to be cleaned, kept it in his pocket, but no, he had given it to Ingrid the evening of the same day, and she had worn it and left it on her dressing table. Now, how did Muriel Tasker find that out?'

Crisp looked blank.

Angel said, 'She found out from her husband, James. And how did he find that out?'

Crisp looked just as blank.

'Because he must have seen it there for himself. He had been in Ingrid Gumme's bedroom. He too had been "at it" with Mrs Gumme.'

Crisp didn't look blank anymore.

'Ingrid made the same overtures to James Tasker as she had to Horace Makepiece and, in her plan, had made an effortless transposition of James Tasker for Horace Makepiece. Tasker was much weaker and far more needy than Makepiece, so it was a doddle. She arrived at The Feathers, must have been after ten o'clock. James Tasker was already there, boozed up and angry and haranguing Gumme about the way he had treated him. He took little persuading by her to pursue her murderous scheme. She had already taken her husband's gun from his drawer in his study. When Spitzer parted from Gumme and angrily went up to his room, Ingrid appeared and enlisted Tasker to transfer Gumme from The Feathers to the Bentley. She drove the car, while Tasker, sozzled in alcohol and egged on by promises of money and whatever else, made by Ingrid, shot him dead through the heart in the back seat. Ingrid then drove the car to the Town End Bridge where they dumped him over the bridge followed by the wheelchair into the River Don.'

'What about the gun? They didn't throw that over as well?'

'No. To perpetuate the idea that her husband was murdered in the hotel by Spitzer, Ingrid needed the gun to be found somewhere in The Feathers. She probably knew that public lavatory cisterns are one of the favourite places police search. So she drove Tasker back to The Feathers to hide the gun in the Gents.'

'Original, sir,' Crisp said. 'Nasty but original.'

Angel nodded.

'The day after, to remove all possible traces of the murder, she and Tasker took the Bentley out into the wheat field early in the morning, and set fire to it.' Then Angel added, 'And the plan might have worked if it hadn't been for the lift at The Feathers being out of order.'

'Wow!' Crisp said, his eyes shining. 'She couldn't anticipate that, sir. Nobody could have.'

'No,' Angel said with a sigh. 'Well, you can finish this off, Crisp. You know everything now you need to wrap up this case.'

Crisp's eyes glowed with anticipation.

'Yes, sir.'

Angel arched his back, pulled a face and sighed.

'Before you start, phone Transport. Organize a car and driver for me. I want to go home.'

* * *

Mary was all smiles that evening. Glad to have him home but no more pleased than he was to be in his own easy chair by the fire. He seemed tolerably comfortable, but, unusually, not very talkative. He couldn't find anything of interest on the television and hadn't any enthusiasm for any of his library books. He ate a light meal Mary had prepared and at seven-thirty with her help, got undressed and into bed. He took the pills and fell straight to sleep.

The next day he didn't hurry to rise. Mary brought his breakfast to bed. He started his ablutions at ten o'clock and was inundated with phone calls from Superintendent Harker, Gawber and Crisp enquiring about different aspects of the cases against Spitzer, Coulson, Ingrid Gumme and James Tasker. The chief constable enquired of Mary into his health and promised to provide anything in his power to hasten his recovery. The Police Federation representative rang about his personal insurance. Ahmed phoned saying that he would be pleased to hear that he had heard that a new car had been ordered for him, also that Mrs Buller-Price had spoken to him and had left a message that she had had Mrs Gladstone to stay overnight and that she thought that she would be all right and would manage satisfactorily while her daughter Gloria was on remand; also that she had baked a special Battenburg cake for him and would leave it at the police station. Even the *Bromersley Chronicle* phoned to ask him about the accident at Bull Foot roundabout and he gave them enough for an eighth of a page in Friday's edition.

There were about half as many calls on Thursday, a mere handful on Friday and then none at all for two weeks.

In the meantime, he had appointments at the hospital and Ron Gawber called for him and transported him and Mary.

Eventually, the plasters were duly removed from his ankle and wrist.

The ankle felt and looked good, but his wrist was out of shape and an unhealthy grey colour, which worried him. After a week's course of treatment in the physiotherapy department, the use came back into his fingers, and they began to have a rosy-pink glow, which delighted him. He took a short walk each day and he seemed to be getting back to normal.

It was now five weeks since he had been in his office and he was beginning to feel the need to get back to work.

He told Mary he was returning to work the next day. She was delighted.

He phoned the office and spoke to Ahmed. He enquired if he had heard any more about a replacement car for him. He said that DS Crisp had taken it and was running it in. He told him to tell DS Crisp to bring it to his house the following morning at 8.20 a.m. prompt.

Then with a light heart, he went up the stairs to set about sorting out some appropriate clothes for the morrow. He went in his handkerchief and sock drawer and at the back found the pack of playing cards and the spectacles that Gumme's son had left with him all those weeks back. He had forgotten all about them, so much had happened.

He put on the black, heavy spectacles and took the cards out of the packet. What Mary had said was true. The cards were not squared up; it seemed that they could not be squared up. Some cards projected the absolute minimum amount, but he shuffled them and looked carefully at them and a big smile spread all over his face. All became clear.

He went downstairs and called out to Mary.

'Want a game of cards?'

'I'm busy. Getting your tea.'

'Come on. Play you at pontoon.'

'You're no good at cards. You can never remember what's gone,' she said wiping her hands on a tea towel. 'Wearing those Groucho Marx bottle-bottom spectacles too?'

He grinned.

'You don't have to remember what's gone with pontoon. Come on. It'll relax you.'

'You don't even like cards. Oh. You've found that stupid pack, have you? It's no good. After you've shuffled them, they don't square up.'

'Depends who shuffles them. Look at them. They're square now.'

He passed them to her. She looked at them carefully. They certainly were. She gave him an old-fashioned look.

'Is this the same pack?'

'Yes. I bet you a fiver I win every trick.'

She grinned confidently. He had never been any good at cards. He hadn't the patience and couldn't remember even a simple sequence.

'You're on.'

She handed him the pack.

They scurried to the table like children and he put the pack down in the middle.

'Cut for dealer,' he said eagerly.

He cut first and showed a king.

Mary reached out and showed a six.

'I'm the dealer,' Angel said, with the grin of a Cheshire cat. He picked up the pack and dealt two cards each on the table.

Mary looked at her cards. She had the five of clubs and the eight of spades.

Angel showed the ace of diamonds and the king of spades.

'Banker's pontoon,' he crowed. 'Pay five-card tricks only.'

Mary said, 'Twist.'

It was the ten of spades.

'Five and eight and ten, that's twenty-three. You're bust.'

He swept up the cards triumphantly and placed them under the pack, and dealt out another two cards each.

Mary showed her cards to be the seven of hearts and then the three of clubs.

'I'll buy one,' she said. 'For a pound.'

Angel grinned and gave her a card.

She turned it over. It was a three of diamonds.

'That's thirteen,' she said. 'I'll twist.'

It was the ten of hearts.

Angel grinned again.

'You're bust.'

He swept up the cards and put them back under the pack in his hand.

This went on for an hour, Angel winning every game, Mary getting angrier and angrier.

Eventually Angel teasingly said, 'These are the cards you said were no good.'

'Let me have a look at them, then.'

She reached out and took the pack from him.

'Are these the cards that that awful man Gumme used?'

'Yes.'

'Is there something special about them?'

'Yes.'

She turned them over face side and looked at the order of the cards. It told her nothing.

'These are the cards that *you* shuffled and wouldn't square up. *You're* one of a particular group of card player that Gumme could never have played with.'

'Why?'

'Because when you shuffle, you divide the pack into approximately two, don't you? Then turn them round and filter them back into one pack. Well, his particular scam would

230

have been defeated by that sort of shuffle. He used to watch all his opponents before a game to see if they shuffled in that way; if they did, he wouldn't play against them.'

'I don't know what you're talking about,' she said, handing him back the pack impatiently.

'Well, look at the pack. It's all squared up, isn't it?'

'Yes.'

'Well, let's take a card. Any card will do. The top card. I take this card, turn it round and put it back in the pack the other way round and you can feel it . . . only just . . . projecting out of the pack very slightly . . . you can feel it as you run your hand long the edge of the pack.'

He handed the pack to her.

She felt the pack and nodded in agreement.

'How's that happened, then?'

'Well, he has had the pack deliberately trimmed. The long sides have been guillotined so that the short sides are very slightly different lengths, making the cards the shape of a trapezium, which means if a card is inserted the "wrong" way the dealer can instantly feel the card projecting out of the pack, and it is easy to slide out to deal at will. What a delight for a card sharp! That's the secret. They *look* exactly the same. The cut is so small. It's something you *feel* not *see*.'

'I think that's rotten,' Mary said. 'You've cheated me! You couldn't lose.'

Angel smiled.

'Yes, Mary. Don't you see? That's why Gumme was called "The Man Who Couldn't Lose".'

THE END

THE JOFFE BOOKS STORY

We began in 2014 when Jasper agreed to publish his mum's much-rejected romance novel and it became a bestseller.

Since then we've grown into the largest independent publisher in the UK. We're extremely proud to publish some of the very best writers in the world, including Joy Ellis, Faith Martin, Caro Ramsay, Helen Forrester, Simon Brett and Robert Goddard. Everyone at Joffe Books loves reading and we never forget that it all begins with the magic of an author telling a story.

We are proud to publish talented first-time authors, as well as established writers whose books we love introducing to a new generation of readers.

We won Trade Publisher of the Year at the Independent Publishing Awards in 2023 and Best Publisher Award in 2024 at the People's Book Prize. We have been shortlisted for Independent Publisher of the Year at the British Book Awards for the last five years, and were shortlisted for the Diversity and Inclusivity Award at the 2022 Independent Publishing Awards. In 2023 we were shortlisted for Publisher of the Year at the RNA Industry Awards, and in 2024 we were shortlisted at the CWA Daggers for the Best Crime and Mystery Publisher.

We built this company with your help, and we love to hear from you, so please email us about absolutely anything bookish at feedback@joffebooks.com.

If you want to receive free books every Friday and hear about all our new releases, join our mailing list here: www.joffebooks.com/freebooks.

And when you tell your friends about us, just remember: it's pronounced Joffe as in coffee or toffee!